"Something sm

Arley said brightly, fro...

...

and the window. Soon Suzette would be struggling by with the box of kittens. If Ben happened to glance out, all would be lost.

"Would you like to join me for dinner?" Ben asked.

"Unfortunately, I can't." She leaned against the sill, hoping to appear casual and block the view at the same time.

"There'll be plenty," he said.

"No, thank you." Arley was struck by Ben's eyes. Such eyes couldn't belong to a cruel man. Maybe she should just throw herself on his mercy.

"Don't you need to use the phone?" he reminded her before she could say anything.

"Oh, yes." How could she have forgotten her supposed reason for being here? It was a good thing she hadn't decided on a life of crime. Her heart was thumping as if she was trying to smuggle diamonds, not kittens.

Virginia Hart comes from a family of writers. Her sister writes mysteries, and her husband—who's even more romantic than Virginia's "heroes"—is an award-winning country-music songwriter. Virginia, not to be outdone, has written mysteries, historical romances, Westerns and now Harlequin Romance novels.

Books by Virginia Hart

HARLEQUIN ROMANCE

Don't miss any of our special offers. Write to us at the following address for information on our newest releases.

Harlequin Reader Service
P.O. Box 1397, Buffalo, NY 14240
Canadian address: P.O. Box 603,
Fort Erie, Ont. L2A 5X3

PET PEEVES
Virginia Hart

Harlequin Books

TORONTO • NEW YORK • LONDON
AMSTERDAM • PARIS • SYDNEY • HAMBURG
STOCKHOLM • ATHENS • TOKYO • MILAN
MADRID • WARSAW • BUDAPEST • AUCKLAND

ISBN 0-373-03272-2

Harlequin Romance first edition July 1993

PET PEEVES

CHAPTER ONE

"NO PETS," Arley groaned, as the red-lettered sign in front of her small apartment building came into view.

The sign's very size would have alerted passersby that it meant business even if it hadn't received top billing over the ones boasting about the pool, microwave ovens and central heating.

In the shadowy reaches of her mind she'd known the sign was there. She must have seen it the day she'd first visited the apartment, and again when she'd moved in. Undoubtedly the words were repeated on the lease she'd signed.

She hadn't noticed. Why should she? She hadn't had any pets. But that was then and this was now.

Beside her on the seat was a cardboard box. Inside the box were two adorable, squirmy little kittens.

This was the second time she'd slowly circled the block, trying to decide how to get her precious cargo into her apartment without being seen. She might have known Ben Travis—building manager, owner and enforcer of the rules—would be waging his regular Saturday battle with the ivy on the front lawn, his chocolate-brown hair in damp disarray over his glistening forehead, as he wielded his sickle with a vengeance.

Strikingly sun-tanned, and impressively muscled, he worked shirtless, his cutoff jeans slung low on his narrow hips. He presented a picture that had given her pause when he'd started earlier that day, and still would have, if she hadn't had other priorities now.

When she'd gone out and given him a chirpy good-morning in return for his brisk one, she'd been struck by how much he looked like Jungle Jake, the hero in the computer program she'd introduced that week at Garfield Junior High.

Fearless and undaunted, Jake fought his way through treacherous swamps, swinging via convenient vines over the heads of snarling predators—all to help the ninth graders of St. Louis find algebra more palatable.

It was easy to imagine Mr. Travis doing that, as he came to the rescue of a beautiful maiden.

Except for one thing. He was evidently an animal-hater and, as such, wouldn't be in the jungle in the first place. Besides, people who didn't care for animals probably didn't have much regard for people, either.

A tiny mew yanked Arley's attention back to the box, and she reached over to retrieve an orange ball of fur with legs, just as it teetered on the edge of the cardboard carton and plopped down beside her.

"Patience, baby," she crooned, resisting the impulse to press the kitten to her cheek before setting it safely out of sight. "Just a little longer and I'll give you a nice saucer of milk."

It was unusually warm for June. Arley's shoulder-length ash-blond hair stuck to the back of her neck. If she'd known how her shopping trip would turn out, she'd have drawn it back into a no-nonsense ponytail. But then, how could she have possibly suspected she'd find herself a prisoner inside her car, unable to turn on the air-conditioning? As welcome as an icy blast might have been to her, she wasn't sure how it would affect the fur-coated foundlings. She didn't want them to catch a chill.

If only "Jungle Jake" Travis wasn't such a creature of habit that he had to work outside on Saturday mornings come hail or heat wave. Why wasn't he sitting in front of the tube watching baseball or something?

If only she hadn't decided to go shopping that morning, something she rarely did on weekends, what with the crush of shoppers. If only she hadn't decided to check in back of the store for a cardboard box to use for her upcoming audiovisual presentation, everything would be fine.

She might be inside, ogling her attractive landlord from her upstairs window, as she'd done the last two Saturdays since she'd moved in, wondering why he'd been so standoffish and musing that although he looked great, he was probably too conceited to make the effort worthwhile.

If only, if only, if only.

Another mew from the box tweaked her conscience, and she regretted instantly what she'd been thinking. If she hadn't gone shopping and if she hadn't checked the bin, she wouldn't have rescued these two little angels that some unspeakable jerk had tossed away like so much garbage.

What would have happened to them?

Uh, oh. Ben had stopped working. He was swiping his forehead with one arm and glancing toward the street. Calm down, she chided herself. He'd been far too intent on his work to see her pass before. If by chance he did, he probably wouldn't recognize her car. There was nothing to set hers apart from the other toy-size gray cars in the neighborhood.

He'd suppose she was a prospective tenant. The building was attractive and the location was handy. Lots of people stopped to look, even when they saw the No Vacancy sign.

As she sat there, torn by indecision, sunlight struck her full in the face, and she saw Ben lean forward. Maybe he couldn't see her features clearly at this distance—she knew he wore glasses sometimes—but he'd certainly spy the gleaming fall of her golden hair and recognize her as the occupant of Apartment E, upstairs front—Arlene Gordon. Arley, for short.

He raised his sickle and dropped it again. Probably wondering why she'd just stopped in the middle of the road, when there was room in front of the building for two cars. This was where she usually parked, even though she had an assigned space in back.

He touched his fingers to his forehead in a cowboy-style salute, obviously meant to serve as a greeting. Why did he have to pick today of all days to be neighborly?

Ever since she'd moved in, she'd wondered how to attract his attention. Her friend, Suzette, who lived in the building and had told her about the apartment in the first place, thought that because he was an artist and a property owner, he probably considered himself a few notches above the peasants he allowed to populate his manor house.

But Arley didn't believe he was like that.

While not effusive, he'd been friendly when he'd showed her the apartment, and again when they were in the office as she signed the lease.

He hadn't flirted or anything, but then business was business, and friendship was friendship. It was always better for everyone if the two were kept separate.

And maybe he just wasn't interested.

A drawing table was set up in front of the wide-open window of his downstairs apartment. She'd seen him there every day when she came home from work, hunched over it in concentration.

So far, he hadn't even glanced at her. Oh well, she'd decided. So be it.

Omigosh. He was coming over to the car. Blood rushed to her head. Her pulses started an erratic rat-a-tat. With delayed reaction, she jammed her foot on the gas. The car lurched back and forth twice before jolting ahead, just as Ben Travis reached the curb.

Through the rearview mirror, she saw him stop short, his friendly smile frozen in place.

She turned the corner and pulled over to the curb, waiting for her heart to stop hammering in reaction to the close call.

But had it really been a close call?

Why should she assume Ben would be so unrelenting about the kittens? He wouldn't expect her to drown them. He'd probably say they were cute, and agree that she was doing the right thing. What harm could these little creatures do to his property? They'd only be there for a few days until she found homes for them.

He wasn't an ogre. She was sure of that. She'd always been good at reading people and would have sensed the meanness behind his smile if there'd been any. His smile had intrigued her from the first day. It was reflected in his eyes and remained there even when the rest of his face was serious. It was a smile that appeared to accept people for what they were, without making judgments.

He had a nice face, too. She liked the crisp, subtle curl in his dark brown hair. She liked his short, straight nose and his frank gaze. She liked his full, show-me mouth and the way he talked, as if he wouldn't be able to communicate if he didn't supplement the spoken word with elaborate gestures.

She liked his loose-limbed walk and the perfect dent in the middle of his squarish chin. In the past two weeks, being something of a dreamer, she'd even allowed herself some fantasies in which she was privileged to plant a kiss there. She liked a lot more about him, too. But all that was beside the point; good looks and a great smile didn't mean he was nice.

Unfortunately, this was true of a lot of people. Her high-school principal, a man she'd detested, had always smiled, especially when he was doling out demerits and other choice penalties. Eric—the good-looking man she'd come chillingly close to marrying—had always smiled when he was conning people into selling their cherished homes to make room for rows and rows of jerry-built apartment complexes.

He'd even smiled when she told him she couldn't take his cutthroat way of doing business any longer.

And he'd continued to smile while assuring her she'd be back once she realized just how good a catch he was.

Then there was her father, the master of the pretending-to-be-what-you-aren't school. As she was growing up, neighbors and friends were always telling her how lucky she was to have such a super dad.

"He has a great sense of humor," they'd say. "He must be a laugh a minute."

Ha! She loved him, and he had a lot of good qualities. But fun-loving, he was not. Thoughtful, he was not. The smiles and jokes were reserved for outsiders, not his family. A career soldier, he'd expected his children to leap to attention when he spoke, just as his troops did.

No, she couldn't take a chance on her landlord. Suppose he said, "Get rid of 'em or you're out on your tail."

He wouldn't. He couldn't. But what if he did?

Arley closed her eyes and rested her head against the back of the seat, breathing in and out, in and out, until she felt in control again. Then she drove around the block and parked in the alley, figuring she could carry the kittens up the back stairs while he was busy out front with the ivy.

So far, so good. The alley was clear. No one was at the trash cans. She eased out of the car, got a firm grip on the box, then pushed the door shut with a hip.

"Hey, there," someone called from above her. "Need any help?"

Ben? She swallowed hard. Were there two of him? Because one was on a ladder now, square in the middle of the breezeway.

Yesterday, she'd overheard the postal worker in Apartment F calling Ben's attention to a sagging drainpipe and reminding him of what might happen if they had a rainstorm. When she'd distracted him from his war against the ivy, he must have decided to do those repairs now. To get to her apartment, she'd have to pass under that ladder, giving him a perfect view of what she was carrying.

"No, thanks. I'm fine." Her voice broke, as she dipped her head over the box to discourage an escape attempt.

"What've you got in there?" he asked. "It looks heavy."

"Not at all. It's just books."

"Not many things heavier than books."

"These aren't. They're, uh, pamphlets for one of my workshops."

He hooked his hammer onto his tool belt, leaving his hands free to grip the ladder as he started to climb down. "Let me help you."

"No! Don't." Her heart began its bongo beating again, as she realized how desperate she'd sounded. He'd suspect something. "I, er, don't want you to stop working because of me."

He grinned and stepped down a rung. "I don't mind."

"But I do. I'd feel terrible." She took several skittering steps backward, in the direction of her car. "Stay where you are. I—I have a terrible cold. I don't want you to catch it."

"I haven't had a cold in years."

"That would make me feel even worse. You know, being responsible for you losing your record."

Obviously puzzled, he shut one eye. "I wasn't trying for a world record."

"But I don't want any help. I feel that, in this day and age, women should bear their own burdens, don't you?" Cringing at the dated sound of her hopelessly lame excuse, she readjusted her grasp on the box, swayed, and almost knocked over a potted *Ficus benjamina.* "I pride myself on my independence."

He shifted his weight on the ladder rung and paused before speaking. "I wouldn't want to rob a woman of her fight for independence."

"Thank you for your offer, though," she said, relieved that he didn't press her further.

"What about your students? Aren't you afraid they'll catch those dastardly germs of yours?"

"What students?" What was he talking about? She raised one side of the box to sabotage the orange kitten's determined climb, then coughed explosively to cover its frustrated meow.

"You're a teacher, aren't you? You work for the St. Louis school system."

"No, no. That is, yes, I do. But I'm not a teacher. I'm an AV specialist." Keep calm, she chided herself. Breathe evenly. Think of sunshine and cloudless skies.

"What's that?" He raked his hair out of his eyes with his fingers. "AV?"

To her consternation, a car roared up behind her in the alley. A door slammed and someone got out. Another one of the tenants? She'd be surrounded. If she was going to escape without Ben uncovering her secret, she had to act quickly.

"Does it really matter?" she asked, breathless from the exertion of struggling with the box.

He frowned, obviously not accustomed to being cut off. "No, I guess not."

She adjusted her grip again. "I don't have time to talk now, and from the look of things, you don't, either. You're probably anxious to finish that drainpipe."

"Right. It could rain cats and dogs any minute," he said wryly, throwing up one hand to shield his eyes from the rays of the dazzling afternoon sun.

Her breath caught in her throat. Had he seen the kittens? Was he teasing her?

"Well..." Half expecting him to point an accusing finger at her, she took another step backward.

"Go ahead." Digging a few nails from a box, he clamped them between his lips and pulled out his hammer. "Don't let me hold you up."

"Hey, what do we have here?" someone said in a resonant, TV commentator's voice.

Before she could make a decision, let alone act on it, Jonathan Fitzpatrick, the insurance adjuster who lived in Apartment A, stopped beside her and peered into the box. She would have recognized him even if she hadn't seen and heard him. His shaving lotion was strong enough to anesthetize a rhinoceros.

Maybe that was the idea. According to Suzette he was a self-styled ladies' man who wouldn't take no for an answer from any female—of any age, size, or coloring.

Whirling around to face him, she put her back to Ben, who, thank goodness, was still on his ladder. "Just books," she said, raising her eyebrows several times in quick succession—Groucho Marx fashion—

and twisting her face into an expression of exaggerated pleading.

His blank stare lasted far too long for comfort. She could almost see the gears rotating inside his head. But then he actually seemed to get it and smiled knowingly. "Uh-huh. Right. Books. Need any help carrying them?"

"She's an independent woman," Ben called from his perch, his hammer upheld in readiness. "Besides that, she's contagious."

"She's what?" Jonathan looked uncomfortable.

"I have a cold," Arley explained.

"Oh." The insurance man straightened his silk tie and smoothed his sandy, salon-coiffed hair into place with the heel of one hand.

"A summer cold can be devilish. I'll keep my distance, too, if you don't mind."

"I don't mind at all."

"Uh, happy reading, then," he said, favoring her with a conspiratorial wink before walking away.

"Are you just going to stand there?" Ben asked, obviously miffed. "Your arms must be tired."

Had she been too brusque in her agitation? "I was trying to decide what I should do."

"About what?"

This wasn't going to work. He sounded suspicious. If she went into the building, he might come down the ladder and follow her, anyway. The situation called for retreat.

"Actually, I've changed my mind about taking these things inside." She tried for breezy enthusiasm. "I'll need them for my workshop on Monday. Why make two trips?"

"Good thinking." His hammer fell and fell again, with more vehemence than necessary.

"I want to thank you," she called over the racket.

"What for?"

Good question. "For... for offering to help me."

Unable to hear his grunted reply, she slid into her car and sped off in search of a telephone booth.

"SUZETTE?" Arley wasn't sure. The voice of the woman who answered the phone had a breathy, Marilyn Monroe quality.

"Who's this?"

"Arley."

"Why are you calling when you're only a few steps away? And why are you whispering?" Suzette sounded more like herself now that she knew who her caller was.

"I didn't know I was. I called because I need your help." Arley waited for her friend's reaction. "Are you there?"

"What kind of help?"

Nothing like having a friend you could count on, she thought grimly.

She and Suzette had met two years before, when Arley had gone to the Flying Carpet travel agency, where the other woman worked, to arrange a sorely needed vacation. The two had hit it off immediately. Suzette, delighted by her own colorful spiel about the beauty of Lake of the Ozarks—and about the preponderance of eligible males who would be there fishing and enjoying the great outdoors—had decided to sign up for the tour, as well. They'd been friends ever since.

Suzette was a lot of fun, but she wasn't one to put herself out for another person—especially if that person was female.

"I'm not home," Arley said. "I'm at a phone booth on the corner of Logan and Whipple."

"What are you doing there, for Pete's sake?"

Taking a deep breath, Arley told the story about looking for a box at the supermarket, and finding two shivering little kittens huddled together under some discarded heads of lettuce.

"What's your problem?" Suzette hooted. "Take them to the animal shelter."

"I did. But as I was going in, there was a woman coming out, and she told me June is kitten month."

"What does that mean?"

"The shelter is overrun with kittens. The chances these babies will be adopted is practically nonexistent."

"You said they were cute."

"They're adorable. But it wouldn't matter if they had solid-gold eyelashes. There are too many kittens and not enough homes."

The long silence indicated that Suzette was thinking. "You said you needed my help. To do what?"

"To get the poor things into my apartment without Ben seeing them."

"No way. Do you know how many times I've moved in the past three years? It's sheer hell. And I like this place. I like the people and I like Ben Travis. Give that part about liking Trav four stars."

Arley tapped the telephone dial absently with one finger. "You don't suppose there's a chance he'd make an exception to his No Pets rule?"

"I don't think he'd make an exception for his own mother. Listen, Cookie, a couple of months ago a guy with goldfish wanted to move in, but Ben refused him."

"You're kidding."

"Nope. And Mrs. Ebert in Apartment G was going to get one of those electronic devices to scare off burglars.... You know, someone triggers it and a tape recording of a barking dog starts up? Luckily she told Trav first, because he nixed the whole idea. I wouldn't be surprised if he sent out an edict that none of us can watch 'Lassie' reruns."

"He doesn't look that hard-hearted."

"So, why don't you run back to the shelter before they close for the day? I've got to go. I just washed my hair and I'm dripping."

Breathing a deep sigh, Arley glanced into the box she'd set beside the phone booth. Even with the windows open, the car was too hot for the kittens. They'd given up their attempts at getting out for the moment and were curled up together, sleeping. One of them was snoring. How could she blithely hand them over to a stranger, knowing what their fate would be?

"Wait," she cried, before Suzette could hang up. "About that help I need you to give me. Ben is on a ladder in the breezeway between the rear entrance and the pool."

"So?"

"So, all I want you to do is distract him. Get him off the ladder and into your apartment on some pretense. Tell him—"

Suzette's laugh was insinuating. "If I ever get that gorgeous hunk of manhood into my apartment, you won't have to tell me what to say to him. But this isn't the right time. Didn't you hear me? I just washed my hair. I won't let him see me like this.''

Arley rolled her eyes heavenward. ''Then come down here and meet me. You can sneak the kittens in, while I distract him.''

''I'd be an accessory.''

''This isn't a bank robbery, Suzette.''

''No, but I've got about as much to lose. After all, Trav owns this place, and a rule *is* a rule.''

''Suzette, who lends you money when you run out before the end of the month? Who comes after you when your car breaks down? Who calls the travel agency and makes excuses for you when you don't feel like showing up?''

''You do. But this is above and beyond the call of friendship.''

''And who isn't going to do those things anymore if you don't help her out when she needs you?''

There was a long pause. ''I get the picture,'' Suzette muttered grudgingly. ''Where did you say you are?''

''The corner of Logan and Whipple. Get here as fast as you can.''

''Oh, all right. But something tells me I'm making a terrible mistake.''

''And, Suzette?''

''What now?''

''Don't stop to blow dry your hair. We're roasting.''

CHAPTER TWO

"HI," ARLEY CALLED cheerily, as she approached the ladder and Ben again.

Her unexpected reappearance caught Ben off guard and he lost his hold on the box of nails he'd just opened. It plopped onto the roof, face down, showering nails into the bed of shasta daisies below.

"Look out," he managed belatedly through clenched teeth.

"I'm sorry."

"It's okay." Judging by the expression he wore, it wasn't. But in the interest of congenial tenant-landlord relations, he'd probably decided not to say so. "Could you pick up a few of those nails and hand them to me?"

In other words, as long as she was here, she might as well make herself useful.

"I'll be glad to get all of them," she said amiably. "They wouldn't have fallen if I hadn't startled you."

"Three will be plenty. I'm almost finished." He waited, but she didn't move. "When were you planning to do this?" he finally asked.

"Oh." One hand fluttered to her mouth in a gesture of confusion, and she cast a furtive look over her shoulder, praying Suzette could carry off her part of their plan. "Soon. But I—I wonder if you could help me first."

He followed her gaze with his own. Earlier he would have leapt to the ground and answered her request for assistance with a resounding yes. Now he clearly thought she was playing games. "What did you have in mind?"

"I'd like to use your telephone."

"Don't you have one?" He obviously wasn't going to make this easy.

"Yes. But mine's out of order."

He studied her for a moment. "The door's unlocked. Be my guest."

That was no good. "I'd rather you went with me."

"It's perfectly safe. The bogeyman's away for the weekend. And I don't have my land mines set."

Her smile was without foundation and faded quickly. "But later, if something was missing..."

Missing? Now why had she said that? He'd think she was some sort of a kleptomaniac. Worse, he'd assume she was trying to flirt with him—and not doing a very good job. At least he'd be half-right.

He looked down at the scattered nails again. "If something turned up missing, I'd know where to find you, wouldn't I?"

"Please. Can we—" She didn't finish the question. "What about your cold?"

She hesitated. "I realized I don't have a cold, after all."

"What is it then?"

"An old allergy of mine returning."

"Hay fever?"

Why was he asking so many questions? "No. Yes. Something like that."

He pressed his lips together and shook his head. "Give me a few minutes to finish this and—"

"I don't have a few minutes. This is urgent."

She'd pushed him too far, she thought, as his eyes narrowed. He'd tell her to darn well wait until he was good and ready—or worse, he'd direct her to the nearest public phone booth.

"Okay," he said, instead, climbing down.

She clasped her hands together to control their trembling, as she heard a car. It was too soon. What was Suzette thinking of? Ben would spot her. They'd agreed she'd wait ten minutes. Could so much time have passed?

"Hurry," she prodded, as Ben pulled the ladder away from the wall and slapped the side to bring the upper portion down against the lower.

"I can't leave this unattended. Some passing kid might get ideas."

"No, of course you can't. I didn't mean to sound so demanding, but a friend of mine was injured in a motorcycle crash." Arley felt called upon to explain the emergency. "I have to phone the hospital to find out how she is."

She was telling the truth, to some extent. One of her audiovisual assistants, a college girl who kept track of the files and sorted the microfiche, had been riding on the back of her boyfriend's motorcycle and there'd been a collision. The accident had happened several days before, though, and the girl had never been in any real danger. Still, better a part truth than a downright fabrication.

Or was she just rationalizing, because she disliked lies so much, even when they were told out of desperation? But people like Ben forced others to lie. The kittens had probably been abandoned in the first place because of the too-often-prevailing No Pets edict.

"The few minutes I'll take to put this away won't make much difference to your friend. I remember how tempting a ladder was when I was little."

"Me, too," she agreed.

"That doesn't surprise me," he said. "In spite of your fragile look."

"Fragile?" She was five seven in her bare feet, and while she had a firm, slim figure, she only kept it that way by harnessing her obsession for chocolates.

"No insult intended. I was only making an observation." He fluttered one hand toward her. "That smooth, ivory skin. That fine-boned face. Those slender fingers, with their shiny pink tips. I think 'fragile' is the right word."

"The fingernails didn't come that way," she teased, trying to camouflage her embarrassment at being so scrutinized. She'd never known a professional artist before. Maybe they all talked this way—as if everything and everyone was a potential subject. "I use polish on them."

He didn't smile. "I can squint my eyes and see the little girl you were. Hanging by your knees from the monkey bars in the schoolyard, not caring that your dress went over your head and showed your ruffled panties. You never cried when you skinned your knees—which was often—but when your feelings were hurt, you ran off by yourself and wept."

"How can you tell all that?"

"You remind me of a girl I had a crush on in the third grade. I can't remember her name, but I remember how good I felt when she smiled at me."

"What happened to her?"

"She accepted my collection of bubble-gum wrappers, then romped away with another boy, whose parents were putting in a swimming pool. When I objected, she told me I was stupid to chew so much gum. That I probably had about two million cavities."

Arley laughed at the little-boy look of surprise he feigned. "So she broke your heart and you turned to art for consolation."

"Maybe." His eyes shone when he laughed, she noticed. "I never thought of that."

A car door slammed and Arley stiffened. At any moment Suzette would appear. "Please, hurry."

"This friend of yours is female?" Ben asked, as she trotted after him into the garage where he set the ladder sideways against the back wall. "And she was riding a motorcycle?"

"What's wrong with that?"

"Just asking."

The smell of garlic and oregano tantalized her from the moment they entered his apartment. Something was simmering on the back burner of his compact stove. He went over to stir it, while she looked around for the telephone she was supposed to be eager to use.

Oh, no. Suddenly she realized the window next to the stove overlooked the alley. Suzette would be struggling by with the box of kittens. If he happened to glance out, all would be lost.

"Something smells delicious," she said brightly, sailing over to wedge herself between Ben and the window. Uninvited, she took off the lid, ignoring his puzzled expression and sniffed the steamy, pungent sauce, elbowing him to one side in the process. "Spaghetti tonight?"

"How can you tell?" He shot a meaningful glance at the pasta on the sink board and the strainer beside it.

When his sarcasm sunk in, her face warmed again. Her skin would be rosy now, instead of the pale ivory he had described before. "A lucky guess."

"Would you like to join me for dinner?"

She was sure the invitation had been offered only because her words had unintentionally sounded like a hint. But she was tempted to accept, anyway. The idea of spending some time with Ben to perhaps change the less-than-favorable impression he must have of her, or better still, get to know *him* better, was appealing. It had been a long time since she'd found herself so intrigued by a man.

"Thank you, but I can't," she heard herself saying.

"There'll be plenty. I rented a John Wayne movie from the video store, *The Searchers*. We'll sit back, watch it, and make pigs of ourselves."

"No, really." She leaned against the sill, hoping to appear casual and block the view at the same time.

Suzette was still in the alley. From the look of things, she couldn't figure out how to angle the box to get through the gate. Or maybe she was afraid she'd break one of her purple-painted fingernails.

"Why not? We don't have to see a Western, if they're not to your taste. I have a pretty fair collection of films, if you want to browse through the titles. Whodunits. Deathless romances. Even a few horror flicks." He raised an eyebrow. "How about *The Curse of the Cat People?*"

"What did you say?" She blinked.

"*The Curse of the Cat People.* A black-and-white film from the forties. Full of dark shadows and guaranteed to make you shiver."

Arley took a deep breath before she spoke. "No, thank you."

"You don't like scary movies?"

"I'd rather not give in to the spaghetti dinner. I'm trying to lose weight."

"Whatever you have to lose doesn't show." He opened the refrigerator and took out a can of beer. "Want one?"

"No, thanks, I'm..."

"... trying to lose weight," he finished for her.

She hated beer, but saying so would be ungracious. As they stood considering each other, she was again struck by his eyes. They were a lighter shade of brown than she'd realized. Milk chocolate, not bittersweet. Such eyes couldn't belong to a cruel man. There was something about his mouth, too, that implied caring. Hadn't he been concerned about children climbing the ladder and getting hurt?

Maybe she should forget what Suzette had said, take a chance and throw herself on his mercy. She'd explain about the kittens, apologize for all the intrigue, and they'd laugh together over her foolishness.

She'd accept his dinner invitation, and though she didn't care much for Westerns, she might find herself enjoying this one, sitting on the scruffy, but comfortable-looking couch beside him, her problems solved.

Wake up, Arlene, she chided. What about the goldfish Suzette claimed he wouldn't allow? Such a person wouldn't be stirred by little kittens or people's rights.

No. The word 'landlord' applied very well to him, appearances to the contrary. He'd probably taken the ladder down because if anyone fell on his property, he could have a lawsuit on his hands.

She bit her lower lip. There was a shuffling sound outside, as if the box had become too heavy for Suzette, so she'd set it down and started to drag it. Had Ben heard? Yes. He looked toward the door. Would he go to investigate?

She coughed several times in quick succession.

"Are you okay?"

"Fine. You, uh, you like John Wayne movies?" she asked, trying to distract his attention from the noise.

He nodded. "I always have. There's a kind of mathematical simplicity in cowboy tales that takes me away from the everyday."

"I suppose that's true," she said, listening for telltale sounds.

"Don't you need to phone the hospital?" he reminded her.

"Oh, yes." How could she have forgotten her supposed reason for pulling him away from his work? Groaning inside, she moved over to the phone.

It was a good thing she hadn't decided on a life of crime. Her heart was thumping so hard you'd think she was trying to smuggle a stolen cache of diamonds into her apartment, instead of kittens.

Grateful he was several steps away, she dialed a number and held the receiver tightly against her head. "Do you have a Vickie Crain registered there? Yes? I'll wait." She paused for what she hoped was a believable length of time. "Hello."

Though she made the pretend conversation as brief as possible, the line was cut off after the third recitation of the time and she ended up talking to a loud dial tone.

"Is your friend all right?" Ben asked after she hung up.

"They think so. But they won't have the results of all the tests until tomorrow."

Oops. He'd put on a shirt and was standing next to his drawing board. Surely Suzette would have made it through the passageway by now, but she could still be on the outdoor stairway leading to the second floor. From this angle he'd have a clear view of her.

"I think I will have that beer," Arley said quickly, trying not to think of the sour smell that always reminded her of an uncle who inevitably reeked of the stuff. When she used to offer her cheek for his hello and goodbye kisses, she'd had to hold her breath to keep her stomach from lurching. The experience had left her with a dislike of beer she'd never been able to lose.

"Help yourself." Ben looked at her quizzically. "You'd rather I got it?"

"Please."

"I'm beginning to think you have a princess complex," he said, sauntering over to the refrigerator. "You like to have a man wait on you."

"Not at all. You're the host, after all, and I don't know my way around your apartment."

He snorted. "Right. I wouldn't want you to get lost."

"You're very good," she said, feigning interest in the paintings that hung here and there on the walls, while actually peering surreptitiously out the window.

Yes, Suzette was at the bottom of the stairs. She'd seen Arley, too. Instead of doing what she was supposed to be doing, though, she was gesturing wildly, signaling that she was having a hard time with the box.

"How do you mean?" Ben questioned.

"Your work. I especially like this one." She indicated the painting in front of her, barely glancing at it. The exuberant splashes of yellow and green probably characterized his style. "Your use of color is imaginative."

He thrust the beer at her. "I wish I could take credit for that one. The original was done by a guy named Vincent van Gogh. Ever heard of him?"

"Oh?" Arley looked back at the painting, then, embarrassed, pressed a hand to her mouth. "Of course."

"I can tell you don't teach art appreciation."

"No, I don't."

"Actually I don't care much for van Gogh, but my sister gave me that print a few years back. When she was here for a visit last month, I hauled the thing out of the closet for her sake."

She nodded her understanding. She'd never been a van Gogh fan, either, but she couldn't say so now. "That's your work on the board, though, isn't it?"

"Right." He waited for her comment.

"Very original."

"Thank you."

"You have an interesting way of..." Something in his voice made her study the drawing for the first time. It was all red and blue lines, like those on a road map. Except this was no road map. "What is it?"

He took a long drink of beer and touched her shoulder. The spot where he touched began to burn. "The female genitourinary tract."

"Oh, I see. It's very, um, very..." She didn't know what to say.

"Thank you."

"I thought you were an artist," she said, feeling somewhat exposed as they looked at the drawing together.

He squared his shoulders. "That's a fairly typical comment I get from people who see my work. My sister, in particular."

"I'm sorry. I didn't mean—"

"Really, Ben, can't you create something beautiful once in a while?" he said, in a voice an octave higher than his own, in obvious mimicry of his aforementioned sister. "Have a display of your work somewhere fabulous, with wine and cheese and important people saying good things about you in the newspapers? You used to draw such nice pictures when you were little. We all thought you were going somewhere."

"I only thought—" Arley tried again.

"So I did go somewhere," he cut in, raising his beer can in a mocking toast. "From Chicago to St. Louis. I do medical illustrations for textbooks and brochures. And I enjoy my work. Not only that, it pays the mortgage."

"I meant that when Suzette told me you painted, I thought you were a real artist."

"What do you call that?" He gestured toward his drawing board. "Finger painting?"

"I'm sorry." Again she'd said the wrong thing.

Exasperated, he closed his eyes briefly. "No, I'm sorry. I always overreact when I think of the smug expression my brother-in-law wears whenever my sister voices her opinion of my work."

"I didn't realize—"

"It's okay. I get the same reaction from everyone. And I guess it's true. Unless I take the time off to drift and dream and paint something that comes from my heart—which I plan to do eventually—I'll never have a showing of my work at a gallery. Meanwhile, I like the challenge in what I do."

An upstairs door closed, opened and closed again; Suzette's agreed-upon signal that all was clear.

Arley sipped her beer and waited until the queasiness in her middle settled. "I want to thank you for your help."

"Anytime."

She glanced toward the stove. *"Bon appetit."*

"Are you sure you won't join me for dinner? I usually invite a new tenant to share a meal with me."

"You do?" She cast him a narrow look, wondering why Suzette hadn't been crowing about the meal they'd shared.

"No," he admitted. "I'm starting a new policy. With you."

She returned his smile and pretended to inspect one of her "shiny pink" fingernails.

It was time to leave. Past time. She'd admired this man's smile from afar, but up close, it was lethal. How could it bring her blood to the boiling point, while giving her goose bumps at the same time?

As Mr. Spock said, it wasn't logical. Her body responded to that smile here, there and everywhere.

And the thought of kissing the man who was smiling at her was mind-boggling.

When he opened the door, she ducked under his arm, and he sniffed. His eyes swept over her and settled on her mouth. "Your hair smells like summer flowers.

"It's the shampoo I use," she said, aware of her voice sounding as if she was having trouble breathing. "Good night, Mr. Travis."

"Ben," he corrected.

"Good night, Ben." If he offered the invitation again, she might accept in spite of herself.

"Good night?"

The question in his farewell didn't strike her until she'd reached her door. She let her head fall to one side in frustration—it was only two o'clock in the afternoon.

Darn. She'd wanted to make a good impression on him if they'd ever had a chance to really talk. She'd even spent a few spare moments mulling over some clever things to say. Now after her ridiculous behavior, he'd think she was living somewhere in the twilight zone.

CHAPTER THREE

WHEN ARLEY entered her apartment, Suzette was sitting cross-legged on the floor, watching the kittens lap milk from a saucer. "Did you warm it first?" she asked, concerned.

Suzette rolled her eyes toward the ceiling. "Next, you'll be wanting me to burp them." She reached out to stroke a furry head. "The black one is exactly like a kitten I had when I was ten. Wish I could take her."

"Could you?"

Suzette raised a spidery eyebrow. "You know the answer to that question."

The orange kitten was apparently full and feeling adventurous again. He pushed his way through the barricade of stacked books Suzette had made into a temporary playpen and started investigating under the couch.

"No, you don't." Arley scooped him up and pressed him to her cheek. "You're a strong little guy. I think I'll name you Samson. Your beautiful sister can be Delilah."

"You're not going to name either of them anything," Suzette reminded her. "You're going to put 'free to a good home' cards on the supermarket bulletin board. You're going to place ads in the paper.

You're going to call all the animal organizations and see if one of them can help.''

''Am I?'' Arley set down the kitten regretfully. ''I'm not so sure I can give them up. Finding them the way I did makes me feel, well, that I'm responsible for them.''

''You act as if you've never had a kitten before.''

''I've never had a pet of any kind. My father didn't like animals.''

''We always had a houseful. Cats, dogs, turtles. Once we even had a monkey.''

''Lucky you.''

''Oh, I don't know. I was the oldest. I had to do all the feeding and cleaning up after them.''

Arley sighed, remembering how left out she'd felt when she watched her friends with their pets. She would have opted for a few extra chores in return for the companionship of a puppy or kitten. Maybe these babies were meant to make up for those lonely, long-ago times.

Maybe. If she could figure out a way to get around Ben Travis and his ironclad no-pets edict.

Ben. How had he managed to captivate her so quickly, without even trying?

Simply being near him gave her more of an awareness of the differences between a man and a woman than she'd ever felt before—not to mention more of an appreciation of those differences.

Despite the part of her that told her he was mean, she felt guilty for what she'd done. He seemed so nice.

''What's wrong?'' Suzette asked, reading her mood. ''We actually pulled this off. You should be happy.''

''I hate having Ben think of me as brainless.''

"Pay your rent on time and don't make any waves. That's all Trav cares about. You aren't a person. You're a check every month."

Was that so? Perhaps. In any case, she'd keep it in mind.

"Show time." Suzette smirked and glanced at her watch as strains of "My Way" came vibrating through the walls and windows. "Jonathan's right on schedule. Same time every night."

"Why does he have to play his music so loud?"

"He probably thinks he's doing us a favor. Providing background music, like they do in elevators."

"Some of us could do with a bit of peace and quiet."

"What do they say about music feeding the soul?" Suzette donned a mysterious expression.

"Or about breaking eardrums."

"Fear not. Trav will get him trained to polite society eventually."

"You think so? Ben has to go over at least once a night to remind him to turn down the volume."

"On second thought, maybe you should invest in earplugs." Suzette swept an arm over her head and rose from the floor, using the action, as she used everything, dishwashing to vacuuming, to practice the ballet she'd taken as a child and hoped to take again when she found time. "I gotta go. My hair is a disaster, thanks to you and your four-legged friends. I don't know if—"

Three sharp knocks at the door cut her off in midsentence. Suzette's blue eyes widened. "Are you expecting someone?"

Arley shook her head.

The knocks came again, louder this time. "Arley?" a male voice called.

"Who's there?"

"Ben," came the booming response.

Suzette threw her hands to her face in horror. "Pretend you're not home."

"How can I? I've already answered."

"Don't open the door. He'll see the kittens. He'll see me."

Arley put her mouth close to the crack in the door. "I'm not dressed, Ben. I was about to take a shower. What do you want?"

"Throw something on and open up."

"He knows," Suzette hissed. "He knows. He's going to want to search and when he does—"

"Just a minute," Arley called to Ben, trying to remain calm in the face of her friend's hysterics.

"Could I climb out the window?" Suzette whispered frantically.

"Don't be ridiculous. We're on the second floor. Where's Samson?"

"Under the couch, I think. I'll get him."

"Hurry."

"Arley?" Ben called again. "Is everything okay?"

"I'll be right there," she answered, dashing into the bedroom to get her kimono.

"I can't reach him," Suzette moaned from her position on the floor. "He's too far under. What are we going to do?"

"Nothing. Just be quiet." Arley waved the woman out of sight and opened the apartment door barely wide enough to peer out.

Affected by Suzette's panic, she half expected Ben to be holding a search warrant. He wasn't. He was holding her handbag.

"You forgot this," he said.

Great. Ben probably thought she was the biggest ditz he'd ever met.

"Thank you." She reached out, then realizing that the gap in her robe showed she was still fully dressed, gathered the silky blue fabric to her chin.

With an amused grin at an action that would have seemed like excess modesty to him, he slid his gaze past her. "I might as well check that window while I'm here."

She shook her head. "Window? What window?"

"The one in the bedroom. You said you like fresh air when you sleep, but some knucklehead had painted it closed. I came prepared." He held up a scraper.

"You don't have to bother. I already fixed it."

"What about the stove? You told me the pilot light keeps going out."

Her pulses were racing. Why was he being so persistent? Was Suzette right? Did he guess that something was going on? No, how could he? He was only being friendly. And evidently he had a mania about keeping things in good repair, which must be why he worked so hard on weekends.

"The stove's all right now," she lied.

His eyebrows came together in an expression of uncertainty. "I'd better check. Just in case. A gas leak is dangerous."

"No, really. The burners simply needed a little cleaning."

A squeak behind her made her gasp. Was it a mew or one of Suzette's heartfelt sighs? Then there was a thump. Suzette must have stumbled over something.

"I didn't know you had company." Ben craned his neck to look around her.

"I don't. Some of the pamphlets probably fell over. I knew I had them stacked too high." She hoped her smile didn't appear as fake as it felt. "You remember, the pamphlets? I decided to bring them in."

"Ah, yes. The pamphlets." He was looking at her oddly.

Hoping to conceal any other sounds, she stepped into the corridor and pulled the door shut behind her. Since he didn't move back, the action brought them so close they were touching. Now he'd be sure to think she was coming on to him, but what else could she do?

Unsettled by their nearness and the need to look up to meet his eyes despite her above-average height, her voice came out breathy, the way Suzette's did when she was talking to one of her boyfriends. "I might as well be honest, Mr. Travis."

"Ben," he corrected again. His voice had changed, too. It had an uncharacteristic gruffness. "I guess you might as well be."

"On weekends, I have a tendency to let things go. I don't pick up or wash dishes or—" she shrugged one shoulder "—or anything. I don't want you to see what a terrible housekeeper I am."

"I've seen unmade beds and dishes stacked in the sink before."

Was he going to insist on coming in? She took a deep breath, then another. So far, this often advised cure for stress hadn't worked for her. But at least the oxygen might go to her brain and help her come up with a more believable excuse.

"I'd rather you didn't come in now. I'm sensitive about the disorder. Besides, I have to take my shower. I've been invited out to dinner, you know."

"Oh?"

It was the only thing she could think of to make him forget he'd come hell-bent to fix whatever needed fixing. "Don't you remember? Spaghetti and John Wayne?"

His mouth dropped. "You said—"

"I've changed my mind. Is the invitation still good?"

"Sure." He pulled at his right earlobe. "But what about your diet?"

"I'll forget my diet tonight and work off the extra calories with exercise."

"What kind of exercise do you do?"

"Walking mostly. When I've eaten a really big meal, I try to do three or four miles."

"My sister's a walker, too. According to her—" he pretended to calculate on his fingers "—at about a hundred calories a mile, it takes thirty-five miles to budge an unwanted pound."

"Something like that."

"There's a basketball court around the side of the building." He jabbed a thumb over his shoulder. "And a ball in the utility closet. Feel free to use it. In fact, we might even work out together some time. A little competition really gets the heart going."

He might not realize it, but when she was in his presence, her heart was already going. She liked his voice. She liked its range, and the way it sounded when he was enthusiastic. As he went on about the value of basketball as a cure-all, she was struck by the way he looked at her. As if he really saw her. And it wasn't insinuating, either. She felt comfortable with him. Or at least she would have under different circumstances.

Now she only wanted him to be gone.

"I wouldn't be much competition for you. Basketball isn't my game."

"I'll give you a few pointers. It's great for working off frustrations. Whenever I'm feeling tired or depressed, I go out and shoot a few baskets."

"That accounts for the thumping I hear under my window."

"Does it bother you?"

"Not at all. I just wondered." She looked down at her hands. "I'd better get to my shower now. Thanks for returning my handbag."

"Anytime."

His fingers brushed hers as he gave her the bag, and darned if the simple action didn't trigger a whole flurry of responses.

"What time is dinner?" she asked, slowly retreating into the apartment.

"How about six?"

"Six will be fine."

"That's early, but we'll need time for John Wayne."

"I'll be there."

"What was that about John Wayne?" Suzette asked once Ben had gone and Arley had slipped into the apartment.

"Ben's rented *The Searchers* and wants me to watch it with him after dinner tonight."

"You're kidding. Do you have any idea how long and hard I've been trying to wangle an invitation out of that man?" Suzette narrowed her eyes. "Maybe I should have done the distracting, after all."

"Do you think I enjoy all this intrigue?"

Suzette crossed the room, opened the door an inch and peered out, wanting to make sure the coast was clear. "I find it hard to believe you don't."

"Well, believe it."

"You haven't had a date since you broke up with Mr. Blind Ambition. I think you'd go out with Godzilla at this point."

"I haven't had a date because I haven't wanted one. I still don't."

"Hmm."

"I'm not crazy about leaving the babies alone on their first night. Besides, I have work to do on the presentation I'll be giving Monday. The last thing I want to do is watch a movie about cowboys and Indians."

"If you mean that, maybe you could make some excuse and tell Ben I'll come in your place." Suzette picked absently at a loose thread on her blouse.

Arley slowly shook her head. "Don't you think it might make him more suspicious than he is already?"

"I guess you're right," Suzette admitted after a few moments.

"Anyway, this isn't really a date."

"A rose by any other name would smell as sweet."

"What does that mean?"

"It's Shakespeare."

"I know, but it doesn't apply here."

"No? Bear this in mind, cookie. I was the one who told you about the vacancy. Without me you wouldn't even be here."

Astonished, Arley stared at her friend. There was an expression she hadn't seen there before. Resentment. Jealousy. A mixture of all kinds of unpleasant things.

"Suzette!"

"Don't 'Suzette' me." She pointed her index finger as if it were a lethal weapon. "In case you discover as the evening wears on that you're actually enjoying yourself, remember—I saw him first."

CHAPTER FOUR

"THAT WAS DELICIOUS," Arley said, feeling that some compliment was expected, though she was actually quite puzzled.

If she hadn't smelled the wonderful aroma or seen the sauce bubbling on the back of his stove, she'd have sworn they'd just eaten the same bottled sauce she kept in her cupboard for the times she wanted a no-fuss meal.

"Thank you." Ben looked properly modest. "Why don't you make yourself comfortable on the couch? I'll stack the dishes in the sink and we'll get down to business."

She pressed her napkin to her lips. What did he mean by "get down to business"? Several mind-numbing possibilities assailed her.

"John Wayne, remember?" He gave her a one-sided smile. *"The Searchers?"*

"Oh, yes." She smiled too. Regretfully, she remembered the speech she had to prepare. "I'd like to stay, but I can't. I brought home a briefcase full of work."

He stacked the plates, set the utensils across them and stood up. "You aren't going to pull a Cinderella on me, are you? The movie was part of the deal."

"Another time, " she insisted, surprised by how difficult it was to beg off, even though she wasn't a Western fan and had passed up that particular movie a number of times before.

Ben had changed into a blue chambray shirt. The sleeves were rolled up to expose magnificent forearms. With it, he wore a pair of oft-laundered jeans that were next door to white. The outfit was plain and unpretentious, the sort worn by a lot of men. Usually she didn't care for the casual look.

So why did she find it stirring now? But then, she'd most likely be stirred no matter what he wore.

Freshly shaved, with his rich, dark hair carefully combed—in honor of seeing her?—and scented with something citrusy, he looked and smelled far more delicious than any meal he could have prepared.

Staying with him to watch the movie was tempting. But the kittens were alone in the apartment and possibly frightened. She'd barricaded them in the kitchen with everything she could find, but was there anything that could hold Baby Samson? He might get trapped while exploring behind the refrigerator or under the stove.

Then there was Jonathan Fitzpatrick. He probably wouldn't tell Ben about the kittens, but he might inadvertently let something slip.

She had to see him tonight, explain her predicament and thank him for not giving her away earlier.

"It's not polite to eat and run."

"I won't. We'll do the dishes before I go."

"Hey." He caught her arm as she started past him. "You told me you were a terrible housekeeper. It's one of the things I like about you."

"Is that a compliment?"

"The first of many." His hold on her arm loosened and slid above her elbow. "That sweater looks lovely on you."

Arley warmed at the compliment. She could hardly believe what she'd heard. Since she'd moved in, she'd wanted Ben to say things like that to her.

"Thank you." With effort, she forced her thoughts back to where they belonged. She was here under false pretenses. Fair play decreed she couldn't leave him with a sinkful of pots and pans. "Shall we get to work?"

"I thought we'd settled that."

"As you well know," she reasoned, "tedious jobs should be done immediately. Otherwise, the thought of them hangs over your head, constantly reminding you of something undone."

"I can take it if you can."

"I'm afraid not." As she took her place at the sink, she glanced at the trash can beside the stove and did a double take.

On top was a jar that had once held spaghetti sauce. There were no other cans or bottles. No tomato paste or purée. No onion or garlic skins. She looked at him questioningly.

"Okay. The cat's out of the bag." He folded his arms across his chest and stood as if waiting for his remark to register with her.

"Oh?" She felt the blood drain from her face at his choice of words.

"You made a confession. Now it's my turn. The sauce was bottled."

"Then what was all that..." She made a stirring motion with one hand, as her heartbeat settled back into a normal pattern.

"There actually was a homemade sauce. I get the urge to fix spaghetti from scratch occasionally, but when I expect to dine alone, I experiment with different herbs and spices."

"You weren't happy with the results?"

He grinned. "The cap came off my jar of oregano, and the entire shebang ended up in the pot. The brew was bitter enough for Macbeth's witches to use in their cauldron."

"What did you do with it?" Arley bit back the giggle that fluttered in her throat.

"'Tain't funny." He scratched his head. "I thought twice about throwing the mess into the disposal. I was afraid it might eat the pipes. When you changed your mind and decided to favor me with your company, I had to dash to the market for prepared stuff."

"We could have put this off until another time."

"And give you an excuse to back out? Fat chance."

She held one of the plates under a stream of water and rinsed it, then picked up another. "Why don't you use a recipe?"

He widened his eyes in mock astonishment. "I, dear lady, am an artiste. I prefer to trust my muse."

"Even if it ends badly?"

"Even if it ends badly." He glared at the door as the music that Jonathan was playing—loudly—changed from Julio Iglesias to something with lots of brass and drums. Ben held up one hand, palm toward her. "Just a minute. I'll be right back."

"Are you going to make a request?" Arley asked.

"Definitely," he growled.

Moments later she heard the knock on Jonathan Fitzpatrick's door and a rumble of voices. Then Ben was back and all was quiet.

"Now, where were we?" He rubbed his hands together.

"We were about to wash the dishes." She thrust a towel at him.

"That's what I was afraid you'd say."

As they worked, Ben talked about the circumstances that had made him choose a career in medical illustration and the ups and downs of free-lancing, as opposed to being employed by a single company. She told him about her job, too, and how a surprising number of parents were against their children learning with computers.

"They seem to think teachers will sit back, drink coffee and gossip, while machines teach their kids. They don't realize these programs actually leave the teachers free to spend more time with each student."

"And your job is to convince them of that?"

"Exactly. It's very satisfying to see a father enter the classroom, ready to defend the way he learned the three Rs, then watch him change his mind and even beg for a turn on the computer he'd previously been damning."

Arley thought that tonight had been satisfying, too. It was odd how such tedious chores as washing dishes was actually fun, when she was with him. Seeing him as the enemy was becoming more and more difficult.

She had to clear the air between them—if she could.

"Why do you dislike animals?" Though she'd phrased the question as nonchalantly as possible, there was something jarring about it.

"What makes you think I dislike them?"

"The No Pets sign in front of the building. What else could that mean?"

"The sign was there when I bought the place."

"But you didn't take it down."

"Actually, I believe that dogs have no place in the city. They belong in the country, where they can have room to run."

"And you think that since few people can afford to own a country home, the rest of the population should be denied the companionship of pets? That the millions of leftover animals should be—should be..." She thought of Samson and Delilah and couldn't make herself say the words.

"This is a free country. If people want animals, they can find an apartment that allows them."

"Have you ever tried to find one?"

He shrugged. "I don't have a dog."

"And you don't want one."

"Dogs and I have never gotten along. Who knows why? One even bit me when I was a kid. I had to have stitches."

"So you've taken this hard line about animals because some dog bit you a long time ago? How many human beings have bitten you, figuratively, over the years? Does that make you hate all humans?"

"Look." There was an edge to his voice. "A person has the right to choose who and what lives in his house."

"And to hell with the rights of those who have to abide by his rules."

"To *hell* with?" He questioned with a hard stare. "Speaking of biting, what bit you? If you like animals so much, why don't you have one?"

She fought to control herself. The exchange between them had brought back an almost forgotten childhood incident. When she'd been eleven, a little terrier pup had followed her home.

It had been a skinny and scruffy-looking thing, with huge pleading eyes. When she'd reached down to check its collar, it had licked her hand.

She'd begged her father to let her keep it. She'd promised everything from making straight A's on her report cards for the rest of her school-going days, to washing his car for a year.

He'd refused and wouldn't even allow the puppy into the yard while she searched for an owner, or for that matter, drive her to the animal shelter where the poor little thing might have had at least a tiny chance of being adopted. The creature had fleas, he'd said, and then proceeded to chase the pup away.

It was struck by a car right before her eyes. Remembering what had happened then caused her to get too emotional. If she wasn't careful, she'd give herself away. Then she'd never be able to convince him to allow the kittens to stay.

Not only that, she liked him. He didn't seem to be a cruel, inconsiderate person. He probably just didn't understand how important pets were to some people.

"I didn't mean to jump on you," she said. "That's a subject I feel strongly about."

"It's okay." He reached over and touched her arm.

Was it really okay? she wondered. The mood had been broken. The warm and special feeling that had built up between them had evaporated. Maybe it was just as well.

With some reluctance, she placed her dishrag on the rack. "I have to run now. I'm expecting an important telephone call."

"I thought you said your telephone was out of order."

Oops. The person who said you needed an excellent memory to lie knew what he was talking about. "I fixed it."

"*You* fixed it?" He whistled through his teeth. "Windows. Stoves. Telephones. You're a handy gal to have around. Maybe I should consider hiring you. As a super."

"Sorry. I have more than enough to keep me busy."

All evening, she'd studied Ben surreptitiously, and one of the things she'd discovered about him was that he wasn't as big as he'd first seemed. Her ex-fiancé, Eric, who worked out with weights three times a week, was bigger, though she'd sometimes mused that if she stuck a pin in one of his arms, he'd fly around the room like a deflating balloon.

No. Ben had a marvelous, broad-shouldered body he'd probably inherited from a broad-shouldered father. His strength obviously came naturally.

"Are you patriotic?" he asked suddenly.

She thought for a moment, wondering what had inspired the question. "I guess I am."

"You believe in all the great American traditions, then?"

"Yes."

"So you'd fight to protect a man's right to a good-night kiss?"

She stopped breathing. "The good-night kiss isn't an American tradition. I'd say it's universal."

"Whatever. I believe in it."

If he'd simply taken a kiss, instead of talking about it, she wouldn't have become tense. As it was, anticipation began to build inside her to the point of explosion. Her forehead felt moist, and there was a dampness between her breasts.

Unsettled, she glanced at his drawing board, wanting to find a topic that would sidetrack the conversation until she regained her equilibrium. "What's that?" she asked, not caring.

"That's the lymphatic system."

"I see."

"And the sketch underneath is the abdominopelvic cavity." He bent down to press scorching lips to the side of her neck.

Her senses screamed, and without meaning to, she leaned into the kiss. "I don't suppose a woman has any secrets from you."

"Nope. I can see right through her." He nudged her head to one side and evened things by kissing the other side of her neck.

It was then that Arley knew she was too much of a coward to continue this. Sidling away, she reached for the doorknob and, feeling somewhat safe, turned toward him to offer him a handshake. "You don't have to see me to my door. You're probably busy on this . . . this . . ."

"If I don't walk you to the door, do I still get mine?"

"Your...what?"

"My good-night kiss."

"Wasn't that a kiss? Two, in fact?"

"That was only a buildup for the real thing."

"Do you always ask permission?"

"Why not? There isn't much pleasure in a kiss that isn't freely given." He thought for a moment. "No. Given is the wrong word. It implies a favor."

"And you don't want any favors?"

"The beautiful princess rewarding with a kiss the knight who's fought a dragon on her behalf? No, thanks. A kiss should be shared." He paused, his breath burning her lips, then barely brushed her upturned mouth with his.

"Ben," she whispered. Was she begging him to continue or asking him to stop? She wasn't sure.

Leaning closer, he slid both arms around her and gathered her against his chest. It was only a feather-light touch to start, then the pressure increased. Not until she heard her own sigh did Arley settle against him and allow her eyelids to close.

For less than a second she wondered if she'd parted her lips or if he'd done it himself. Then she stopped thinking. Pulling only a fraction of an inch away, he moved his mouth, allowing her a breath—although she wasn't sure she needed it. She wouldn't have been surprised to find that he had the power to do the breathing for both of them.

"I'd better go," she heard herself saying. *While I still can,* she added silently.

He didn't answer. He was stroking her hair and gazing at her. "How many little boys' bubble-gum wrappers did you make off with when you were eight?''

"Good night." She backed away from him. "Thank you for . . . a delicious meal. I'll have to reciprocate."

"Good word, reciprocate. Tomorrow night?"

"No, not then."

"When?" he asked, catching hold of her hand.

"I'll let you know." Twisting her hand ever so slightly, she succeeded in freeing herself from his grasp. "Good night."

Halfway up the outer stairs that led to her apartment, she stopped and looked back. Ben's door was closed but his draperies moved slightly. Was he watching her? No. Why would he?

She waited a few more seconds to be sure, then backtracked as quietly as she could to Apartment A and tapped on the door.

"Hey, what have we here?" Jonathan Fitzpatrick wore a cranberry-hued shirt made of a shiny fabric that fit like a second skin. Around his neck was a chunky gold chain with a lion's-head pendant. His smile seemed to show all thirty-two teeth.

His apartment had so much white, a person could have ended up snow-blind. The walls, the long, curving couch, the shaggy carpet that almost covered the shiny wood floor. Only the asparagus-green throw pillows and the colored splotches on a giant canvas over the glass table in the dining alcove added color.

"I didn't mean to intrude," Arley said hesitantly, catching a glimpse of a woman seated on the floor in front of the white stereo cabinet sorting through tapes.

"Pardon?" Jonathan shouted to be heard over the tape player.

"You're not intruding," the woman called, raising a hand in greeting. It was Suzette. She wore a backless Hawaiian-print sundress Arley had never seen before and had done her hair in a new curly style that made her look entirely different. She held up a cassette tape and said something Arley couldn't hear. Then quite clearly she called, "Your tête-à-tête over already?"

Arley nodded and turned to Jonathan. "I only wanted to thank you," she yelled, although she realized she had little chance of being heard.

"What's that?" He cupped one hand around his ear.

"I said, I wanted to—" She broke off. Making him understand was impossible. "I'll come back another time."

"'Never put off...'" he quoted, not bothering to finish. He took her elbow and led her into the white kitchen. The swinging door fell into place behind them, shutting out some of the noise. "First of all, what's your pleasure?"

"Nothing, thanks."

"A nice cool drink'll relax you and give you the courage to say whatever you wanted to say to me."

Was he suggesting she'd been harboring a secret yearning for him and had been too timid to say anything? "No, really. I wanted to thank you for not giving me away to Ben. The kittens, remember? I don't intend to keep them, but I'd rather he didn't know they were here. He might object."

"I haven't squealed on the others. Why should I squeal on a cutey like you?"

"The others?"

"Yeah. There's a regular pet underground in this place. I'm probably the only tenant without a furry companion."

"And Ben doesn't know?"

His laugh was like that of a naughty child. "That's the beauty of the situation. He thinks he's on top of everything. You know, strictly enforced rules. No booze by the pool. No laughing after ten o'clock. Next there'll be a bed check and lights out at eleven."

"Who else has pets?"

"Oh, the old woman in Apartment D, for one. Dora, is it?" He said the name through his nose, imitating Dora Shelby, who lived across the hall from Arley. "She has two, maybe three, cats. Lovey Bear and Pansy Puss. Can you beat those names?"

"I've seen the stuffed ones in her window."

"Stuffed, my aunt fanny. Those stuffed ones are camouflage in case off-with-their-heads Travis happens to look up when the real ones jump onto the sill where they can be seen."

"You're sure?"

"As sure as I am that you have one of the cutest little tushes in the city." He leered at her to reinforce his dubious compliment. "She only lets 'em on the sill when the sun shines against the front of the building. Then there's a glare that helps the illusion."

"You said there were others."

"Yeah, there's the retired couple in Apartment G— the Eberts?" Jonathan was holding her shoulders now, moving his fingers in a mini-massage designed, no doubt, to thrill the curl from her hair. "The couple who looks scary enough to haunt houses? They have poodles.'' He guffawed. ''Smoke would pour from Travis's ears if he found out.''

''How do you know about them?''

''I thought everyone knew, except for Travis, that is. God, I resent his type.''

''What type is that?''

''The type who can afford to buy property, and lords it over those who can't. Poor working stiffs like me. Elderly people who need the companionship of animals to bring some love into their lives.''

People like the Eberts, who could haunt houses? Arley wanted to ask, not taken in by his sudden sympathy act. Whatever his reasons, she was still grateful that he'd gone along with her.

''Jonathan,'' Suzette called from the next room, ''don't you have 'Evergreen'?''

''I'd better go,'' Arley said.

''You wouldn't break my heart, would you?'' His little boy expression came complete with a pouting lower lip.

Give me a break, she thought. Didn't he ever abandon his come-ons? They must have been exhausting. ''I doubt I'd be doing that,'' she said.

''I'll drop by one day and, uh, borrow a cup of sugar. I'll bet you have a lot of sugar.''

''I try to keep some on hand,'' she said, removing his fingers from her shoulders, one by one, then walking into the other room.

Now the trick was to exit without offending him and making a dangerous enemy. With the brightest smile she could muster, she waved at Suzette to let her know she was leaving. Only a few steps to the door and she'd be free. What was that smell? Incense?

She'd almost made good her escape when three sharp knocks announced another visitor.

Suzette sprang to her feet and threw the door open to a furious Ben Travis. "Hi," she cooed, throwing her head back in a way that brought a mass of springy curls across her forehead. "Come in and join the party."

Arley froze. A dash back into the kitchen would have only called more attention to her presence, and it was too late to drop to her knees behind the couch.

"I'd like a word with Fitzpatrick, if you don't mind," Ben said, trying unsuccessfully to sound congenial. "I spoke to him earlier about—" He broke off abruptly when he saw Arley.

His stare said it all. Now he knew her excuse about expecting an important telephone call had been a lie.

Evidently Jonathan saw Ben's shock and decided to do a bit of needling. He moved forward and slipping an arm around Arley's waist, pulled her along with him. "What can we do for you, Travis?"

Ben jerked his attention away from Arley. "Do you want to step outside?"

"That sounds ominous. Do you plan to resort to fisticuffs?"

Suzette giggled, and Jonathan cast a smug look at her.

"I thought you might not want your friends to hear what I have to say." Ben's voice sounded so cold Arley barely recognized it.

"I have no secrets from anybody here."

"As I've told you many times before, normally you would have had to agree to a few ground rules before you moved in, but I inherited you from the previous owner.''

Jonathan snapped his fingers. ''Don't tell me. I forgot to listen for 'Simon says.'''

''This racket you call music disturbs the rest of the tenants.''

''Is that all?''

''No. I've also had complaints about the Sunday afternoons you and your friends monopolize the pool, making the others feel unwelcome, and then not picking up your trash when you leave.''

Jonathan glared at him. ''I'll take the matter under advisement.''

''That would be a good idea.'' The calmly spoken words held a clear threat. ''Starting immediately.'' He turned away and started back down the hall.

Jonathan slammed his door shut rudely. ''Now you see what you got yourself into when you moved into this firetrap,'' he told Arley, shaking his head.

''Yes, I see,'' she said, too miserable to waste time arguing with Jonathan.

Should she dash out and explain to Ben why she'd been there? Why she'd lied about leaving him early?

No. How could she?

The kittens were curled up together, sleeping, when she let herself into her apartment. Delilah stirred and opened one eye. Satisfied all was well, she closed it again and began to snore. Arley stood and watched the pair for long moments.

''How could anything so adorable cause so much trouble?'' she asked aloud.

With a sigh, she walked into the bedroom, wriggling out of her sweater as she went. Was Ben thinking about her, or had he already become absorbed in his movie about the conflict between cowboys and Indians? Did his interest in the Old West mirror his personal philosophy? One side always right, the other always wrong?

In a week or so, when she'd found Samson and Delilah a new home, maybe she could try to take up where they'd left off tonight. Taking a page out of Jonathan's well-worn book, she could always "borrow a cup of sugar."

But did she want to?

Was Jonathan right? Not about the loud music, of course. He was definitely out of line there. But did Ben enjoy playing lord of the manor, setting up rules his peasants had to follow—or else?

She remembered well how quickly all playing had stopped when her father came home. She could still hear her mother's nervous warning, "Pick up your toys. Your father doesn't like them in the living room. And don't tell him you were playing with the Jackson girl. He doesn't like her family. Sit up straight. Comb your hair. Is that your good dress you're wearing? Your father won't approve."

She recalled too, how relieved she'd felt the day she'd moved into her own apartment. How different things were once she was away from his influence. Then, father and daughter got along just fine.

Of course, he didn't live in the same state now, which helped. When he'd taken his retirement, he and Arley's mother had moved to Oregon. According to him, it was the only place to live.

Did Ben's no pets policy mean he, too, was a tyrant who brooked no opposition? That he was uncaring about the needs of others? Would he actually give poor Dora Shelby notice if he knew about Lovey Bear and Pansy Puss?

Arley had to find out. And if it was true, then no matter how she felt when she was with him, no matter what his kisses did to her, she wanted no part of him.

At least, she'd do her darnedest to convince herself of that.

CHAPTER FIVE

NERVOUS ABOUT her orientation class on Tuesday and how her newest project would be received, Arley spent the rest of the weekend and most of Monday in preparation. It was worth it; everything went smoothly.

She had a full house. All the attending teachers had experience with microfilm readers, and the operation of the new ones weren't that different. When the session was over, participants wandered around the coffee room, where Arley circulated talking about the exciting learning possibilities in the new "magic pencil" that could transfer a child's drawings to a TV screen—and about the two cuddly kittens available for adoption.

Her Polaroid pictures of them drew the expected oohs and ahhs. But there were no takers. In each case there was a spouse who wouldn't approve, or more often, a landlord who didn't allow pets.

There was one nibble, though. The vice-principal from Fairfax High had an aunt who'd recently lost her fifteen-year-old cat. The woman might agree to take a replacement—or two.

"She said no more pets. But you might be able to convince her," the vice-principal suggested. "I'll give you her number."

It was a chance, anyway, and would have left Arley hopeful, except that at the same meeting, she met Mildred Barnes, who had a problem of her own. The woman was a teacher who'd just transferred from another district. After she'd signed the lease and moved into her new apartment, she'd discovered to her dismay that Rags, her little floor mop of a dog, wouldn't be allowed to stay.

"I'm keeping him at a kennel," she said, "but he's miserable being locked up. The prices are outrageous, and my budget is strained to the bursting point. If nobody can help me, I'm going to have to take him to the pound."

"Let me work on it," Arley said, knowing how slight the chances were that she could do anything. Dogs were even more difficult to find homes for than cats.

Her hair had been done in a neat upsweep when she'd left home that morning, but as the day wore on, wisps had come loose to caress cheeks that were damp and rosy. As usual, when she got home, Ben was at his drawing table, and as usual, he looked up as she passed his window. This time, though, he got up and came to the doorway.

"Arley," he called, as she started upstairs.

She stopped, one hand on the rail. "Yes?"

"Don't forget the carpet men on Friday."

"So soon?" She scowled. "I thought they wouldn't be here until next week."

"I'd have thought you'd be saying, 'At last.' That stained carpet must be hard to live with."

"Well, yes, but could they be put off a bit? I'll be working Friday."

"No chance. Yours isn't the only apartment being done, you know. It isn't necessary for you to be here. In fact, the workmen prefer not having an overseer." He sounded annoyed at her attitude, and no wonder. Most tenants—Arley included, under other circumstances—would jump for joy when their landlord kept a promise about installing new carpets and such.

"I suppose," she agreed weakly.

Without saying anything else, he went back into his apartment.

Her knees almost buckled once she'd safely reached her own apartment and stepped out of her shoes. So the carpet would be installed on Friday. What would she do with Samson and Delilah?

There was no point in calling Suzette. Her friend had made it clear she wanted nothing more to do with the cats.

Wait. Dora Shelby. If her carpet wasn't one of those being replaced and if she truly was a pet owner, she might be willing to help in this emergency.

Arley hurried over to knock on Dora Shelby's door, which opened only enough to allow one heavily mascaraed eye to peer out. Arley wasn't even sure it belonged to Dora.

"Hi," she said, trying for an earnest look. "I wanted to talk to you if you have a moment."

The woman glanced over her shoulder. "I—I can't right now. I'm watching my favorite TV show."

"Please," Arley insisted.

"Just a minute." The woman emitted a resigned sigh and closed the door.

After a series of thumps and shufflings from within, she sidled through the door and into the hall, her silver-blue hair disheveled.

"We can talk out here," she panted. "It's so much cooler."

So, Jonathan *had* been telling the truth. From her own experience, Arley recognized the sound of pet owner's panic when she heard it. Mrs. Shelby was definitely a member of the pet underground.

"Are you having new carpeting installed?"

"Why, no. Mine's only six months old. Is that what you wanted to talk about?"

"No," Arley whispered, glancing at the stairwell to make sure no one was listening. "I wanted to tell you that I know about Lovey Bear and Pansy Puss."

The woman clasped her hands to her ample bosom. "I—I don't know what you're talking about."

"It's all right. I have cats, too," Arley said, deciding to take a chance. "And I'm going to need your help."

Dora Shelby grabbed Arley's arm with a surprising show of strength and, without a word, yanked her into her apartment. "How did you find out? Does Mr. Travis know? Oh, what am I going to do?" she asked, as she bustled around fixing a snack.

"Your secret is safe. Mr. Fitzpatrick told me, and he promised not to say anything."

The cinnamon tea Dora served was so pungent Arley's eyes watered, and the chocolate-chip cookies provided calories she didn't need, but Arley accepted the woman's hospitality. Perched on the blue-flowered couch, she looked at reams of animal photographs and listened to the tribulations of housing secret pets.

Dora had two daughters who led busy lives that left no time for her. Her "babies" were her life. This location, within walking distance of the supermarket, the laundromat, a movie theater and a senior citizens' center, was perfect, because she didn't have a car.

"I simply can't move. And where would I go? Nobody lets you keep pets anymore."

"I'm beginning to find that out. That's why I came to you." As rapidly as she could, Arley told her tale, showed her own pictures and explained about the men who'd be going in and out of her apartment.

"Could I impose on you to kitten-sit that day while I'm at work? I'll give you my key and when the men have left, you can sneak them back into my place again."

"I'd be delighted. This is perfect." The woman set her teacup down. "I didn't know what I was going to do tomorrow morning. Now you and I can trade favors."

"What happens tomorrow morning?" Arley was almost afraid to ask.

It seemed that Pansy Puss and Lovey Bear had appointments for shots at eleven o'clock the next day. Dora's daughter was going to pick her up at ten-thirty and drive her to the vet's. The daughter was an impatient woman who expected only to honk and have her mother come running.

"Mr. Travis is always at his window. Watching." Dora frowned. "I don't know how he can be so nice and at the same time, so cruel."

"He isn't cruel," Arley said quickly, feeling called upon to defend him. "It's only a matter of education."

"What do you mean, education?"

"I'm certain he has no idea of the attachments people form to their pets or of the trials they go through to keep them. I'm sure if someone took the time to convince him—little by little—he'd soon see that sheer gratitude makes pet owners the very best of tenants."

"Isn't that the truth? They're so happy to find a haven for their animals they seldom complain about anything and make a point of paying their rent on time."

"Exactly." Arley had never thought about this until she joined their ranks, but people with animals were too nervous about their status to make waves.

"You could be right about Mr. Travis," the woman mused, alternately stroking one, and then the other of the two matching white cats who sat on either side of her.

"I'm sure I am. He'd probably be very reasonable if he were approached in the proper way." Arley set her teacup down. She'd spent too much time here already, considering the mountain of work she'd brought home. "How have you been getting your cats past Ben's window until now?"

"I've been making two trips. Carrying one at a time in my big straw bag. But when you're my age, the stairs get steeper every day, especially since my babies are so wiggly and my arthritis has been acting up."

"Couldn't you have your daughter park in the alley and take them down the back way?"

"She won't do that. That would mean circling around and driving down a one-way street. She disapproves of my babies, anyhow." Dora stood and followed Arley to the door. "You don't have any plans for tomorrow morning, do you?"

"No. My presentation isn't until five in the afternoon."

"I can count on you, then, to draw Mr. Travis away from the window somehow?"

Arley exhaled sharply. "I don't know."

"You scratch my back and I'll scratch yours, as they say," the older woman reminded her.

"How will you get the cats inside when you come home?"

"Caroline Oates will be home by then. She's going to ask Mr. Travis to fix her squeaky kitchen cabinets."

"Mrs. Oates has pets, too?"

"A Siamese cat named Me Too and a Lhasa apso named Qwon Yen. She'll spirit them over to the Eberts' apartment while he's there. Well?" Dora leaned forward. "Now that you're one of us, can I count on you?"

What choice did she have?

"All right," Arley agreed, trying not to think about the puzzled way Ben had looked at her when she'd put up her senseless argument about the arrival of the carpet men. "I'll do my best."

"Now what?" Arley heard Ben growl as she knocked on his door the next day.

He'd been engrossed in his work when she'd passed by his window earlier, but she had to wonder if he was deliberately ignoring her.

When he didn't answer, she knocked again. Before she was finished, though, he threw open the door, apparently ready to tell his unwelcome caller to get lost.

"Hi," she chirped cheerily.

She'd donned a blue T-shirt, trim white shorts that showed her long, shapely legs—no less provocative, she hoped, for being pale—and running shoes.

He concentrated on her face. "What can I do for you?"

"I don't have any classes this morning," she said.

"Oh?"

"So I thought I'd come over for my lesson. Basketball?" she reminded him. "I hope I didn't arrive at a bad time."

"Well..." His eyes glazed over, as though he was trying to remember if they'd set a specific time and date. "I'm working against a deadline. Could we meet at—say, three?"

"I have to be across town for a presentation at five." She sighed regretfully. "But I wouldn't want to take you away from your work."

"It's okay." She'd evidently piqued his curiosity. A brush-off last night. Flirting with him today. "Give me a few minutes. I can always use a break."

"If you're sure."

As he trotted into the bedroom to change, the telephone jangled and he doubled back to turn on a speaker phone. The sudden sweep of his hand knocked over his cup and sloshed coffee onto his drawing table.

"Damn." He snatched up a paper towel and cut off the stream of coffee before it could reach his drawing.

"Travis." A man's voice said through the speaker. "Are you there?"

"Hold on. I spilled some coffee all over my— *Damn.*"

"I'll get it," Arley offered, rushing to tear off another towel. In a sense, this was her fault, anyway. Wasn't everything these days?

"It's Hank Golding, from the Medical Center."

"I know. What can I do for you?" Ben asked, as he went back to the bedroom.

Worriedly, Arley looked at the clock. She should have come earlier. Dora's daughter would be here in only seven minutes.

"You're cutting it close this time, guy," Golding warned. "Less than a week left until the pictures are due."

"I've had some distractions," Ben replied, sticking his head out of the door to be heard.

Namely me, Arley thought ruefully, as she tore off another paper towel.

"Like I keep telling you," the caller went on, "working out of your home isn't a good idea. You should consider taking that office here on the fifth floor. There's lots of light. A coffee machine."

Three minutes, Arley thought, after another glance at the clock.

"Have I ever let you down?" Ben's voice challenged in obvious exasperation.

"No," the man admitted, then went on at length about the psychology of keeping home and workplace separate.

Two minutes.

And then Ben was back, looking like a poster boy for health foods, dressed in cutoffs and a neon-orange tank top. He made a string of glorious promises to the man on the telephone and hung up. "Let's go."

It was Keystone Kops timing, but they made it. A car pulled up in front of the apartment house, and someone honked just as Ben shut his door. He stopped momentarily, but Arley was walking close behind, preventing him from turning back.

Dora appeared at the top of the stairs with Pansy Puss in her arms just as Ben ducked into the utility closet where he kept the ball. The honk sounded again.

"Who's doing all that honking?" he asked, his voice muffled by work clothes and tarpaulins that were draped over storage boxes and bulging plastic baskets.

"Dora's daughter," Arley said, resting her back against one side of the door and her feet against the other to bar his way if he emerged too quickly.

"All set," he said.

"Good. Uh, is that a baseball?" Stalling for time, she pointed to one of the shelves. "May I see it?"

He handed the ball to her and waited. "It's just a baseball I had when I was a kid. Not even autographed. Nothing to set it apart from any other baseball."

"Except that it was yours," she said, her hand closing around his.

An unnatural stillness settled around them. The words and the sentiments, though sincere, were not ones she'd have uttered under normal circumstances. Convention, even in this enlightened age, called for the man to say such things first, if they were to be said at all. Even as he looked at her, she wondered where she'd found the audacity.

He blinked, surprised, and let the ball drop into one of the plastic baskets.

"I meant—" faltering, she searched for an explanation that would soften the impact of what she'd said "—our possessions, just because they *are* our possessions make them special to us and to those who—"

"I heard you the first time." Placing a long arm around her waist, he drew her away from the door, and gave her a brief, hard kiss that curled her toes inside her sneakers.

Abandoning her explanations along with her reservations, she slid her hands over his shoulders, twined her fingers behind his neck—as she'd wanted to do almost from the first moment she'd seen him—and pulled his head down for a second merging of their lips.

"Oh, Arley," he moaned.

Still holding her captive with one hand, he caught the knob with the other and shut the closet door, obviously not caring that the stuffiness in the tight quarters was hardly conducive to romance. Burrowing his face into the softness of her hair, he found her ear and gently nibbled it.

Unless she made a move, though she wasn't sure she could, their basketball game was going to be postponed indefinitely.

A car door slammed in the general direction of the alley. Brisk footsteps sounded on the walk. They stopped at the mailboxes to the right of the closet and there was the scratchy sound of a key turning in a lock.

It was a small distraction, considering the powerful emotions she was feeling, but it was enough to bring Arley back to earth.

"They've gone," she whispered.

"So?" He held her closer.

"The key," she said, indicating the coffee can on the shelf above her head where the key to the laundry room was kept. "Someone might want to do a wash."

"I don't think so."

"Someone might have seen us come in here. It's undignified for a landlord. It could set a terrible example."

"For whom?"

"Your tenants. They might . . . I don't know."

"Impeach me?" His mouth seared the base of her throat before he looked at her again, his eyes black in the dimness of the utility room. "As you say, I'm the landlord. That puts me in the catbird seat, doesn't it?"

"My basketball lesson," she reminded him, turning her head just as his mouth swooped down. It missed its mark and scalded her cheek.

Ben groaned, recognizing defeat. "Just for that, lady—" he slapped a hand against the wall above her head "—I'm going to run your fanny off."

His threat wasn't an empty one. The game they played was fast-moving, and he showed no mercy.

But when she'd learned a controlled dribble and had managed to make twenty baskets—no easy trick for someone who'd squeezed through high school phys ed by being the teacher's gofer—he relented and said they could quit for the day.

"That'll give you time to shower and whip up a quick snack for your coach."

The idea sounded wonderful. But when was she going to whip up this snack? And more important, where? "I have to work tonight, remember?"

"It doesn't have to be anything fancy. An omelet. Grilled cheese." He grinned. "Canned soup?"

"Another time." She dabbed at her face with the hand towel he'd brought for her. "I'm too beat to operate the can opener."

"Peanut-butter-and-jelly sandwiches."

"You expect me to exhaust myself on the court to get rid of calories, then put them right back on again with peanut butter?"

"That wasn't work. That was fun."

"Sez you."

"We could drive over to a fast-food place and get burgers and fries. Your treat, if you insist," he tried again.

"Methinks you're just looking for excuses to avoid your drawing board."

"Methinks you're right." He shrugged one shoulder. "How about later? You'll probably be ravenous after your session. I'll be too burned out by then to do anything creative, and I know a great little café where we can go for a late supper."

Darn. She wanted to go with him. She wanted to sit across a candlelit table from him and listen to him talk. It wouldn't even have to be candlelit. It could be a booth at some diner. She felt herself flush at the thought of him reaching over to clasp her hand. Of him smiling at her. Of their walking up the stairs together—and then, receiving another of his kisses, which was guaranteed to make the world go away, for a time at least.

Perhaps even two kisses. Or three. His arms around her. His hands caressing her...

It couldn't happen. Not yet. Not until she got things straightened out. For when they came home, he would walk her to her door. He might expect to come inside. If she begged off, citing the late hour as her reason— and it would be late by the time they got home—he might insist on checking the pilot light she'd told him she'd fixed. The jig would be up.

"What's wrong?" He dipped his head to gaze at her carefully. "Cat got your tongue?" he asked with mock severity.

Cat.

Her mouth gaped open before she managed to reason away her overreaction to the word. *Steady*, her inner voice warned. Ben had used a common, everyday expression. He hadn't meant anything. "I was just thinking."

"You've decided to accept my invitation?"

"No, " she said soberly. "It'll have to be some other time."

He waited, his disappointment seeming much greater than her refusal to go out with him warranted.

Or was her guilty conscience working overtime?

"Some other time," he agreed quietly.

Then he was gone.

She'd barely had time to step out of her shoes and strip off her T-shirt when the doorbell rang. Was he back to repeat his invitation? Hoping she'd changed her mind? Her heart started a frenzied beat. If he was, could she ask Mrs. Shelby for a second favor? It would mean doing another favor in return, but it would be worth it, tenfold.

"The password is 'Samson,'" someone whispered outside the door, as Arley wriggled into her T-shirt again.

"Shh!" she cautioned, pressing a finger to her lips as she allowed Suzette entrance.

"How could Trav know what 'Samson' means?" Suzette yanked off the towel she had wrapped around her head like a turban.

Arley did a double take when she saw the reddish highlights in the girl's usually black hair, but didn't remark on it. "He couldn't know, I guess. I jump at everything these days."

"You look beat."

"I am beat. I've been playing basketball," Arley said, as she tried to decide whether to pair her gray suit with a turquoise blouse or a white one.

"You've what?"

"Was there anything in particular you wanted?" Arley asked, wanting to change the subject. "I have to get ready for work."

"I was wondering how the strategy worked."

"What strategy?"

"Oh, I forgot." Suzette snapped her fingers. "Remember last night when Travis came to Jonathan's apartment?"

"Yes." How could she forget?

"Didn't he look furious?"

"The music was too loud."

"It was more than that." Suzette spied her reflection in the mirror and turned toward it to study the effect of her newly tinted hair. "Didn't you see his face? I think he was jealous."

"Why would he be?"

"Because he didn't expect to find me there. I was only having Jonathan tape a few songs for me, but Trav couldn't have known that. So I got to thinking. Maybe I've been playing this wrong. I know it's old-fashioned, but then Trav might be an old-fashioned guy. Maybe he likes the excitement of the chase."

"I don't know what you mean." Arley tried to remember if she'd already put everything she'd need in her portfolio. It was getting late. She didn't have much time.

"I, my dear, have agreed to go to a jazz concert with Jonathan Fitzpatrick tonight. What's more, I'm going to a piano bar with him on Friday."

Now Suzette had Arley's attention. "You're kidding."

"He's not that bad once you get to know him. He's really quite good-looking, and he has a great car. Besides, it might set a fire under Trav."

Arley didn't know what to say. In the chaos of the day's happenings, she'd almost forgotten her friend's attraction to Ben. What would Suzette say if she knew about the electricity that had been crackling between Ben and herself? Certainly she'd consider it the ultimate betrayal.

"I don't think such tactics will work with Ben," Arley said slowly. "He's too straightforward."

"You don't know much about men, cookie. Some of them don't know they want something until they see someone else is interested in it."

"Playing games can be dangerous."

"*You* should talk about dangerous games," Suzette accused. "Edna Ebert told me that you've been chosen by the pet underground as the tenant most likely to succeed in brainwashing Trav into allowing pets."

"Mrs. Ebert told you that?"

"She said Dora told her. Everybody's buzzing about it."

"Super." Forgetting her need for haste, Arley sank onto the couch.

"Jonathan says it reminds him of the old fable. You know, where the mice get together and elect one of their number to put a bell around the cat's neck?"

Arley felt as if her heart had dropped to the pit of her stomach. "Jonathan knows about this supposed arrangement, too?"

"He won't say anything. But you better take care. When Trav finds out, all hell will break loose."

"I know."

"You've had a lot going on at school lately. Haven't you made any progress in finding a new home for Samson and Delilah?"

"Not yet."

"What about the woman whose cat just died? The aunt of that vice-principal?"

"I haven't been able to reach her."

"Hmm. Maybe you forgot that you have to pick up a telephone and dial to make a connection. Thought transference won't work."

"I know. I know."

The week should have been a perfect one for placing the kittens in a loving home. Being around all those prospective owners should have meant the odds were in her favor.

Had she really been trying?

She hadn't placed an ad in the newspaper yet or put up any notices in the supermarket. She'd told herself that she was too busy. But was that the whole truth? Or had the hours she'd spent cuddling and playing with Samson and Delilah made her care too much about them to seriously consider giving them away?

Why should that be necessary, anyway? Darn Ben and his rules.

Suzette stepped away from the mirror and gave her headful of now coppery curls a shake. "Do you like my hair this way?"

Arley hesitated, forcing her thoughts away from the warning about Ben's fury if he learned what had been happening behind his back. "Truthfully?"

"Certainly not."

"Then I love it. It's definitely you."

CHAPTER SIX

FRIDAYS WERE always hectic. This one, however, was even more so. Summer vacation was approaching, and parents' night was upon them. This meant many extra hours of running from school to school for Arley, who'd volunteered for the duty before she'd acquired her feline family.

It was almost eight when she pulled into her parking space. Ben had evidently just had a heated discussion with Jonathan and was still standing in front of the closed door of Apartment A looking less than pleased.

As she sailed past, he acknowledged her hi with a preoccupied nod. Midway up the stairs, she realized he had fallen in behind her.

"How'd things go the other night?" he asked.

"Very well," she said, moving more sedately as she wondered if he was watching her walk. Her part of the program had not only been well-received, but she'd almost managed to convince one of the other lecturers he needed a couple of kittens. "What about your project?"

"Almost wrapped up."

"Good."

At the landing, she fully expected him to go straight ahead to see Hal Nordoff, who had most likely been the one to complain about the loud music. Ben didn't continue, though. He turned left when she did and waited while she dug for her key in the jumble of her carryall bag.

"I'd like to see it," he explained, when she looked at him quizzically.

Her throat constricted. What did he mean? Had Dora been caught in the act of transferring the kittens? Did he want a confrontation?

"It?" she echoed.

"The new carpet. I was busy when it was installed, so..." His voice trailed off.

Inside her handbag, she tightened her fingers around her key ring, but didn't withdraw it. If she did, he might insist on opening her door for her.

What was she going to do? If Dora had done as they agreed, she would have brought Samson and Delilah back when the men installing the carpet left. Since Arley now trusted the kittens enough to allow them the run of the apartment, they could be anywhere.

"If you can't find your key, I'll let you in with mine."

"No, please, don't. I'd rather see the carpet alone first. You know, to get the full impact." Her stomach knotted as she realized that the weakness of this argument might well have surpassed her others. "Besides," she added desperately, "the place is a mess."

He put a hand on the wall above her head. "You told me you let things go on weekends. The weekend's just begun."

"I got a head start. I was in a rush this morning and let everything fall here, there and everywhere."

"Perfect strangers saw your apartment today."

"Yes. But as you say, they were strangers. I want everything to look nice when you see it." She was aware that her voice sounded wheedling, but how else could she sound if she was going to be convincing? "I plan to have the furniture gleaming. The throw pillows plumped and inviting, et cetera, et cetera. It's important to me."

His brows came together as if he couldn't decide whether he should be irritated or flattered. "Do you have any idea how much carpeting costs? I think I paid for the right to see what I paid for."

"You will. You will."

She caught her lower lip between her teeth. Clearly, he didn't believe her. Now what could she do? Faint? No, he'd carry her inside and put her on the couch. She could almost hear his bellow of indignation. She could see his pointed finger as he showed her the way to the door with her packed suitcases. Or maybe he wouldn't wait for her to pack. Maybe he'd give her the heave-ho and hurl her things after her.

Unexpectedly, the door of Apartment D flew open and Dora appeared, talking to herself. Omigosh. No. She'd evidently kept the kittens longer than Arley had expected. She was struggling with Samson who wasn't taking kindly to being held. In trying to manage the key and settle him down, the woman hadn't noticed Ben. She was coming toward them, head bent, cooing endearments.

Emitting a sharp cry, meant to serve as a warning, Arley deliberately teetered offbalance, pretending to turn her ankle. When she flung her arms outward to steady herself, Ben obligingly caught her.

"Are you okay?"

"Yes. Thank you." She tried for the grateful sound of someone who'd just been rescued. Still clinging to him, she waited for Dora, who'd finally gotten the message, to retreat. "I'm not used to these new shoes yet."

He glanced at the low-heeled shoes. "They don't look precarious."

"Maybe I'm a little weak. I didn't eat anything today."

"That diet you were telling me about?"

"Yes." Her breathing was shallow. "Maybe I'm being overzealous about it."

"Maybe." Judging from his amused expression, he didn't buy it. On the other hand, he wasn't angry with her anymore. Maybe he'd decided that this, along with all the other inane things she'd done, was simply her way of playing hard to get. He was probably touched that she didn't have any more imagination than to try the same flirting tactics Martha Washington had used on George.

Oh, when all this was over, she'd make it up to him, she promised herself. And then never, ever, would another lie cross her lips. She'd told more fibs in the past few days than she'd told in her entire twenty-six years.

For a moment, she thought he'd kiss her. That kiss, though again the idea defied logic, would make everything all right somehow. He didn't. Instead, he crooked his index finger under her chin, the better to fasten her with a stern look.

"It's all over, Ms. Gordon," he said gruffly. "I'm in charge. Like it or not, I make the rules. If you want to stay here, you'll keep them."

"What do you mean by that?" She tried to pull back, but his other hand held her fast.

"I can't allow you to starve yourself to death on the premises. I'm taking you to dinner."

"I—I can't tonight. I have work to do."

"Yes, you can. Everybody needs a break." The timbre of his voice changed. "Care killed the cat, you know."

Was she supersensitive these days or was Ben mentioning cats more than a person normally would? She couldn't remember ever hearing that particular expression before. Was he making it up? She searched his eyes, trying to tell if the glint she saw there signaled some inner meaning. "I thought it was curiosity," she managed.

"That, too."

"I don't know." She pushed her lip forward contemplatively, her body alive with sensation. Could she go with him? Did she dare? Oh, how she wanted to!

"I can't have you fainting on me, can I?" He tore his gaze from her eyes and moved it to her lips. "Do whatever it is you have to do to make your quarters presentable, and I'll come for you in . . . one hour exactly. No arguments."

Her smile lingered as she entered her apartment and, despite the time limit Ben had placed on her, allowed herself the luxury of standing with her back against the door, relishing the newfound sensations.

Not for long. A gentle tapping beamed her back to reality. It was too soon. Ben wouldn't have had time to get back to his apartment. What was Dora thinking of?

"Hi, neighbor." It wasn't Dora. It was Jonathan Fitzpatrick, holding an empty cup. He was wearing a clinging black shirt and black slacks. His potent shaving lotion made her sneeze. "I came for that sugar you promised me."

Still weak from her close encounter of a horrendous kind, she stood back and let him in. This was all she needed.

"Did you see Ben going down the stairs as you were coming up?" she asked, trying to sound casual.

"As a matter of fact, I did. Don't tell me you've been bending the rules."

Darn. What would Ben think? Or maybe he hadn't noticed which door the insurance man had knocked on. After all, hers wasn't the only apartment on the second level.

"No," she said, though it wasn't any of his business, "I had new carpet put in today, and he wanted to check on it." She took the proffered cup and started toward the kitchen. "I haven't shopped yet this week, so I can't give you much, but—"

"I don't really want any sugar," he interrupted in a voice that sounded as if he had pebbles in his mouth.

"What, then?" She thrust his cup back at him.

"A little conversation."

"Some other time," she said, mentally going through her closet for exactly the right outfit. "I have plans. Come to think of it, aren't you busy tonight, too?"

Suzette had said they were was going to a piano bar. If that was true, they should have left already. Had the romance fizzled this soon? Maybe Suzette had decided that making Ben jealous wasn't worth having to spend time with Jonathan.

"Plans can be changed." One of his eyebrows rose and the other lowered, as if he was trying to look like a "hunk" in a movie magazine. "So how about it? In the interest of being neighborly?"

"I'm afraid not."

This, she didn't need. Ben had given her an hour. Among other things, she had to dash over and ask Dora to kitten-sit some more. Then she had to shower and fix her hair. Every moment counted if she wanted to be ready on time.

Uninvited, Jonathan sauntered across the room and made himself comfortable on the couch. "You should be nice to me, seeing as I know your secret. Sit down. We'll discuss your options."

Arley hardly heard him. In the confusion of the last half hour, she hadn't even noticed the carpet. It was the deep rose she'd sighed over in the book of samples Ben had shown her. The color he'd said he positively couldn't give her because if she moved, it might not complement the next tenant's decorating scheme. It would have to be something neutral, he'd said.

Dear, sweet Ben. That was why he'd wanted to come in. To see her reaction. She'd cheated him out of his fun.

Caught up in her thoughts, her unwelcome guest's suggestion only now registered, and she turned to him. "Are you insinuating that I'd better be friendly or you'll give me away?"

"Just kidding." Jonathan picked up one of the sofa cushions and frowned at a place where the fringe had pulled away. "Would I do that?"

Her first impulse was to catch his wrist, pull him to his feet and haul him over to the door, as she might do to a child who was behaving badly. In the light of his knowledge of the pet underground, though, she chose to be a bit more tolerant. If she could manage to be civil to some of the stone-faced parents she dealt with, she should be able to manage it with him.

"I don't want to be rude, Jonathan, but..."

"What's the matter, neighbor?" His smile looked forced. None of it was reflected in his eyes. "Afraid King Travis will be jealous if he catches me here?"

"Why would he be?"

"Oh, I don't know." Jonathan was obviously trying to seem cool and debonair, but it wasn't working. He brushed his hair back with the heel of his hand and looked around the room. "This is quite the carpet, but it's got me puzzled."

"Why is that?"

"Travis had carpet installed in Apartment C today, too. But it's blah-beige. Like the carpet in all the other apartments. Like mine, before I ripped it out and gave the floor my own treatment. I think that says something about... well, his motives. Don't you?"

If she hadn't been so outraged, she would have laughed at the implication that she would have given herself to Ben to get the shade of carpeting she wanted, or that *he* would have made such an arrangement with her. "Good night, Jonathan. Goodbye, Jonathan. Thank you for stopping by."

"You don't have to act this way."

"You're right, I don't," she said, almost pushing him into the hall.

This time as she started into the bedroom, it was the telephone that stopped her.

"Hello," she said, exaggerating the breathiness in her voice to hint gently to her caller that she was in a hurry.

"This is Mildred Barnes." Before Arley could remember where she'd heard the name before, the woman went on, "I'm calling about Rags."

"Oh, yes." The little floor-mop dog who needed a home. "Is everything okay?"

"No. That's why I'm calling. When we talked at the meeting the other night, you said you might be able to find a home for him."

"I'm sorry. I haven't found anything."

"That's what I was afraid you'd say." The woman sighed. "You were my last hope." Her car-insurance premium had come due, she explained. So she'd had to take the dog out of the kennel and was using a folding baby gate to keep Rags in the kitchen while she was at work. "He's a precious little angel, but he gets lonesome and starts to whine. Not very loud, but enough that anybody standing outside the door can hear him."

"Namely your landlord."

"Right. You remember I told you Rags's original owners just moved away and left him chained in an old shack? He didn't have any food or water, and by the time he was found, he was dehydrated and starving. When he's left alone now, he thinks he's been abandoned again. It's just a matter of time before my building manager finds out, and when he does . . ."

"I know."

"I'll have to take the poor little thing to the pound. What other choice do I have?"

"Hold on a bit longer," Arley said, trying for a hopeful tone. Though she'd never seen Rags, something about his sad history reminded her of the pup her father hadn't allowed her to help. By helping this animal, maybe she could make up for it in some way.

A few of the people she'd asked about taking the kittens had simply said they didn't like cats. They might feel differently about a dog.

"What's the point in waiting? I've exhausted my possibilities, and this isn't your responsibility."

"I know. But keep working on your end, and I'll get back to you."

"If you say so."

She'd have to double her efforts, she told herself, as she raced across the hall to Dora Shelby's apartment. She had a meeting at the junior college scheduled for next week. Maybe if she talked long enough and fast enough, she could convince somebody that with the rash of burglaries, they needed a watchdog.

Did Rags bark much? She'd forgotten to ask.

As she raised a hand to knock, Dora, with a struggling Samson in her arms, threw it open, startling them both.

"Could I impose on you to keep the kittens a bit longer?" she whispered when she was safely inside the other apartment. "I have a dinner date, but I should be back by about eleven-thirty, if that isn't too late for you."

"Is your date with Mr. Travis?" The woman clasped her hands together when Arley nodded.

"Goody. I saw how you two were looking at each other. It'll fit right in with our plans."

"Dora," Arley began, wanting to set the woman straight about what Suzette had told her earlier, "there is no plan."

"Edna Ebert and her husband are overjoyed about your idea of educating Mr. Travis," the woman said excitedly. "Your date tonight will be his first lesson."

Arley groaned and held up a hand in protest. "That wasn't what I meant."

Dora wasn't listening. "I've gathered some animal-rights brochures for you to show him. A couple are about the anguish of pet owners who've had to put their animals to sleep because of heartless landlords. Others explain about what good tenants pet owners can be. I put them on your coffee table earlier."

Animal booklets? Arley shook her head. She hadn't seen them. It was a good thing Dora had told her about them, or else she might not have noticed. Ben might have seen them, though, and wondered.

"Tonight isn't really a date," she explained. "It's something I was forced into when you came out with Samson."

"He doesn't need to know that, does he? We're convinced that before you're through with him, he'll not only allow us to have our pets, he'll throw open his own doors to one of God's voiceless creatures."

"Dora!" Arley groaned. How could so much be going on right under Ben's nose? He'd turn purple if he found out.

"He's the dog type, I think. Don't you? A Dober-man. Or maybe a Labrador. Something he can take jogging with him." Dora put a thoughtful finger to her lips. "I'll check among my friends and see who has a puppy that would be right for him. My goodness. He might even take two."

"Aren't you being a bit premature?"

"No, indeed. As you yourself pointed out, it's only a matter of time before he discovers our secrets, and tosses the lot of us out." The woman's voice broke, and she tried unsuccessfully to blink back tears. "Please. We're counting on you desperately. Lovey Bear and Pansy Puss, not to mention your own little Samson and Delilah. Their fates are in your hands."

CHAPTER SEVEN

THE SHADOWY POLYNESIAN restaurant, decorated with seashells and aquariums and squat candles flickering in green-glass holders, was less than a mile's drive away. From the calming pleasure that encompassed Arley after they'd been tucked into their thatched booth, though, it seemed that nothing less than a romantic moonlit cruise could have brought them here.

There was no music, unless she counted the contentment that hummed inside her as she and Ben sipped slender frosted drinks made of exotic fruits. At first, they barely talked. But the bond between them didn't seem to require words.

Soon they were caught up in spearing, with sword-shaped toothpicks, artfully arranged delicacies from platters that kept coming and coming. Occasionally they erupted in bubbles of soft laughter.

And every so often, when each was tempted by the same morsel or chose the same sauce bowl for dipping at the same time, Ben's fingertips brushed hers. The gentle contact, warm and comforting, touched a part of her that had never been touched before.

Immaculately groomed and shaved, Ben was fuel for any woman's fantasies. He'd worn a tie, although the restaurant was casual. Away from the apartment house and her worries about the kittens, she was able to unwind, talk easily, and learn something about him and the things in his past that had turned him into the man he was.

His family had expected great things of him, he said. When he'd chosen to become a medical illustrator, he'd been made to feel as if he were heir to the throne and had abdicated. He'd been a teacher in an art academy in Chicago, but had quit after only one year, mostly because of his need to create.

"Actually, I played the starving artist for a while. Did the kind of thing my family considered serious work. Street scenes, landscapes. Even made a few sales."

"I'd like to see some of it."

"What you've already seen is my best work. I enjoy the intricacy. The detail. And I feel good knowing that what I do serves a purpose." Absently, he brushed the palm of his hand across her knuckles. "But I'll admit sometimes I see something—" he gazed intently at her "—or someone who sets off a spark inside me and makes me want to reach for my brushes and capture my feelings on canvas."

Needing to break eye contact, she looked down at her plate. "And do you?"

"The assignments that put the spaghetti on the table keep me too busy. But maybe…maybe I will soon. To let me satisfy that other part of my nature." He paused. "Would you consider posing for me?"

"When inspiration strikes you?"

"It already has," he said.

Arley felt herself pulling back, the old need to make excuses returning as she visualized Ben learning her secret and becoming angry with her. "Maybe some-time," she murmured.

He signaled to the waiter to bring them another drink. "Your schedule appears fairly flexible. I don't imagine you'd consider giving yourself a break for three or four days."

"You're right about that. Some of us have employers to answer to."

"I'm going to look at some lakefront property. It'd be a nice drive, and I'll probably stay over for a few days. To get the feel of the land, so to speak. I'd like you to go with me."

"I wish I could," she said truthfully, missing him already.

"You could use the time off." He caught her chin and raised it, pretending to be concerned. "You're a bit pale."

"I'm always pale by your standards. I don't tan."

"No chance in changing your mind?" His eyes glittered with a persuasion that was even harder to resist than his words.

"I can't," she stated with more assurance than she actually felt.

"Okay. Be that way." His fingertips, warm and slightly rough, danced across her hand again, making music inside her. "I'll give you a number where I can be reached. Would you keep an eye on things while I'm gone? And if anything goes wrong, give me a call?"

"What could go wrong?"

"Lots of things," he mused, turning her hand over, as if it were a fine art object he was appraising. "As they say, when the cat's away, the mice play. I'll leave the phone number in your mailbox.''

Their fortunes came in gold-veined tissue paper twisted at the ends like taffy, rather than in cookies. Arley's reminded her—as if she needed reminding— that "love and trust are one." Ben's promised a surprise within a fortnight, a prospect Arley didn't find too comforting.

Tell him now, a small voice inside urged. *You can't put it off any longer.*

"Arley?" Ben asked, apparently noticing the change in her. "Is something wrong?"

Love and trust are one, her fortune said. What about Dora and the Eberts? Her confession would implicate them, too.

"Everything's perfect," she said aloud, crumbling the thin paper into a wad.

Ben glanced at his watch. "We'd better go. Ready?"

"Ready."

Fragrant breezes, previews of the summer to come, lifted strands of her honey-gold hair as he helped her out of the car when they were home. The moon was a crescent of silver in the dark sky. The shimmering stars were waiting to be wished upon. Even the music coming from Jonathan's apartment as they walked past was more tender than raucous.

What was it about Ben? An inexplicable warmth filtered through her when she was with him, and she was certain that such feelings could never exist inside only one person. By necessity they were shared. Could he be the part of the whole she was meant to be?

His caring about what was important to her, wanting to learn more about her, made Eric's obsession for tearing down existing houses and replacing them with high-rise monstrosities seem all the more petty and self-serving.

Everything about Eric, from the way he combed his hair to the car he drove to his choice of hobbies, was designed to improve his image.

"You should have seen me today, Arlene," he'd boast over dinner. "Nobody, but yours truly, could have pried that old lady out of that shack. I convinced her that her daughter would probably let the grandkids stay overnight more often if she lived in a better neighborhood."

Could she actually be falling in love with Ben this quickly? Or was the comparison between him and Eric so marked that her judgment was affected? There hadn't been time yet for either of them to really discover the other's inner self. Was there a possibility that he was keeping as many secrets from her as she was keeping from him? She doubted it.

Ben, unaware of her trickery, was taking her at face value. What would he think, *do*, when he discovered the truth?

"Did I tell you how pretty you look?" he asked once they'd entered her apartment.

Arley smiled in pleasure. She'd worn a green raw-silk blouse that fell below her hips. A wide sash cinched her slender waist and hung in folds at her side. Her pants were green, too, in a darker shade, and she wore several chunky bracelets that served to emphasize the delicacy of her wrists and hands.

Though she'd never taken the initiative with anyone before she'd met Ben, gazing into his dark eyes, she was tempted again. Mentally, she saw herself sliding her arms around his neck, pulling him toward her. She heard herself sighing in chorus with him and felt their hearts beating in unison.

Now, courtesy of Jonathan Fitzpatrick, Natalie Cole was singing the duet she'd done with her father. "Unforgettable." As usual, the volume was turned too high, but Ben didn't seem to notice. Perhaps he was thinking, as Arley was, that the lyrics might have been written for the moment.

"I forgot to thank you," she said, regretfully brushing her fantasies aside.

He closed one eye. "Was that a simple thank-you, or do I detect a dismissal, as well?"

"Not at all. I want to thank you not only for the lovely supper, but for the carpet, too. It looks even more beautiful than I imagined it would when I saw the samples."

"I'm glad you're pleased."

"And I realize that rose isn't a very practical color to have installed in an apartment."

"Nope." Absently, he traced a finger from her elbow to her wrist and back again. "Now you're obligated to stay here. Where would I find another tenant with furniture that would fit into your color scheme?"

"Have you ever read about the psychology of colors? Rose, for example, makes for glowing, happy thoughts."

"So the color of the carpet is making me feel the way I do? Not the woman standing on it?"

Her mouth felt dry. "No. According to the books I've read, it's the carpet."

EE BOOKS!

EE GIFTS!

LAY THE "LUCKY 7" SLOT MACHINE GAME !

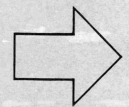

NO COST! NO OBLIGATION TO BUY! NO PURCHASE NECESSARY!

PLAY "LUCKY 7"
AND GET AS MANY AS FIVE FREE GIFTS

HOW TO PLAY:

1. With a coin, carefully scratch off the silver box at the right. This makes you eligible to receive two or more free books, and possibly another gift, depending on what is revealed beneath the scratch-off area.

2. Send back this card and you'll receive brand-new Harlequin Romance® novels. These books have a cover price of $2.99 each, but they are yours to keep absolutely free.

3. There's no catch. You're under no obligation to buy anything. We charge nothing—ZERO—for your first shipment. And you don't have to make any minimum number of purchases—not even one!

4. The fact is thousands of readers enjoy receiving books by mail from the Harlequin Reader Service®. They like the convenience of home delivery . . . they like getting the best new novels months before they're available in stores . . . and they love our discount prices!

5. We hope that after receiving your free books you'll want to remain a subscriber. But the choice is yours—to continue or cancel, anytime at all! So why not take us up on our invitation, with no risk of any kind. You'll be glad you did!

This lovely Victorian pewter-finish miniature is perfect for displaying a treasured photograph— and it's yours absolutely free—when you accept our no-risk offer.

PLAY "LUCKY 7"

**Just scratch off the silver box with a coin.
Then check below to see which gifts you get.**

YES! I have scratched off the silver box. Please send me all the gifts for which I qualify. I understand I am under no obligation to purchase any books, as explained on the back and on the opposite page.

116 CIH AKWM
(U-H-R-07/93)

NAME

ADDRESS   APT

CITY   STATE   ZIP

7	7	7	WORTH FOUR FREE BOOKS PLUS A FREE VICTORIAN PICTURE FRAME
🍒	🍒	🍒	WORTH FOUR FREE BOOKS
⬤	⬤	⬤	WORTH THREE FREE BOOKS
🔔	🔔	🍒	WORTH TWO FREE BOOKS

THE HARLEQUIN READER SERVICE®: HERE'S HOW IT WORKS

Accepting free books puts you under no obligation to buy anything. You may keep the books and gift and return the shipping statement marked "cancel." If you do not cancel, about a month later we will send you 6 additional novels, and bill you just $2.24 each plus 25¢ delivery and applicable sales tax, if any.* That's the complete price, and—compared to cover prices of $2.99 each—quite a bargain! You may cancel at any time, but if you choose to continue, every month we'll send you 6 more books, which you may either purchase at the discount price...or return at our expense and cancel your subscription.

*Terms and prices subject to change without notice. Sales tax applicable in NY.

"Some carpet." He gestured toward the kitchen. "If you're looking for a way to reinforce your thanks, offer me a cup of coffee. Then we'll be even."

The surge of panic that swept through her only lasted a few seconds, which made her want to laugh. She was safe. Samson and Delilah were with Dora. "I'm afraid I only have instant."

"I think I can handle it." He whistled as she clicked on another lamp, illuminating the living room. "How did you manage this?"

"Manage what?"

"When I was here earlier, you wouldn't let me in because your apartment was a mess. Now it's like something out of a magazine."

"Hardly that. But . . . yes, I work very quickly."

"I can vouch for that," he said, but something told her he wasn't just talking about her housecleaning.

Oops. A dozen cans of cat food were stacked on the counter. Beside them was the ten-pound bag of litter she hadn't taken the time to put away. Ben was right behind her.

Had he already seen it?

Clicking off the kitchen light, she whirled around so quickly their bodies came together in a gentle collision. Instinctively, her hands pressed against his chest and then moved to his shoulders. At the same time, his arms went around her waist.

"Why . . . why don't you wait in the living room?" she stammered, fighting the overwhelming desire to make the most of their position and caress the taut muscles beneath his jacket. "I'll serve you."

"What did I do to deserve such treatment?"

"The carpet, for one thing."

"And for another?"

"The carpet is quite enough, don't you think?"

"I'm an old hand at making instant coffee. There are a few tricks that make it taste like it was freshly perked."

"I know all the tricks," she insisted.

"I won't argue about that." He brought one of her hands to his lips and kissed each finger in turn.

Tiny thrills raced down her arm, sending spasms of delight everywhere.

"I've never known anyone like you," he said, each of his words bringing his mouth closer to hers, and his eyes reflecting his desire for her. "Everything you do takes me by surprise."

"I'm sorry."

"Don't be sorry," he whispered against her mouth. "Don't ever be sorry for being what you are."

There was wondrous pleasure in the moist, satiny caress of his lips that followed. In the mingling of her breath and his. And in the coaxing pressure of one of his hands at the small of her back.

But Arley couldn't let things go any further. Not yet. Allowing their relationship to deepen when nothing had been decided about the kittens was only asking for trouble.

Her reasoning sounded ridiculous even to her own ears—something as important as a possible future with Ben shouldn't depend on something so small.

Still, she'd noticed with couples she knew that it wasn't the big problems that weakened their relationships; it was the seemingly insignificant ones.

For now, she had to keep a wall between them. Maybe tomorrow or the next day, she'd find a suitable home for the kittens. They'd be gone, and all this would be over.

Or would it? Did she want to give up the furry little bundles she was beginning to care about? Why should it be necessary?

"If you like, you can turn on the TV while you're waiting," she suggested too brightly, somehow succeeding in pulling away from him. "I'll get the coffee, then we can talk."

Breathlessly, she flew into the kitchen again and closed the door before turning on the light. As quickly as possible, she stowed all the cat paraphernalia out of sight and stood, for a moment, with both hands pressed against the sink, trying to keep control.

When she finally went back into the living room with her tray, Ben was watching a chase scene in a popular detective series.

What's wrong with me? she wondered as the mere sight of Ben, making himself at home on the couch, filled her with tenderness. After great deliberation, she'd bought a couch with three sections—two placed together and the third on an angle across from the others with the table in between—because she liked the coziness of such an arrangement, where friends could talk facing each other.

With Ben settled in the center of the doubled section, his long arms sprawled along the back, it seemed laughingly Lilliputian. It would seem odd if she sat on the section opposite him, yet she wasn't sure she could handle sitting so close to him.

"Smells good," he said, scooting to make room for her and taking the decision out of her hands.

As she set about pouring and stirring, his hand fell to her shoulder with unstudied ease. Then before she could protest, if that had been her plan, his fingers tightened, and he drew her toward him.

He lowered his mouth to her ear, and she was past protesting, past joking and past paying attention to her reservations about him. His other hand held her chin steady, readying her for his lips, which were nibbling their way down her throat and up again, taking a long, agonizing time to collect a proper kiss.

With the contact of his warm, firm mouth—a bare brushing at first that offered false reassurance, then a deepening pressure—she lost all perspective. She could no longer focus on the reason for their differences.

It wasn't only the exhilarating touch that affected her; it was the mingled scents, the wonderful tastes and the giving in to shared longing.

"Are you cold?" he whispered against her ear.

She smiled at the question. Surely he must have known she was cocooned in the all-consuming heat of their actions.

"There are goose bumps on your arms." Sliding down to kiss one elbow, he struck a magazine stand with his foot and toppled it.

In attempting to right the stand, he inadvertently set the casters at the bottom of the couch rolling and ended up on the floor between the sections.

Laughing at his predicament, she offered him a hand. But instead of allowing her to help him to his feet, he pulled her down beside him.

He smoothed a hand along the soft newness of the plush carpet. "You were right. The color is most inspirational."

"You think so?" Melting against him again, she offered no objections when he tugged at her sash and discarded it.

"Definitely."

His hand moved upward under her blouse, scorching her skin, until it reached her lacy bra.

The sigh she emitted as she arched her back, wasn't intentional. But she couldn't have stopped it any more than she could have stopped herself from drawing his mouth down to hers.

"Did you hear bells?" he asked gruffly, his breath caressing her throat.

"I don't know." She waited, while he felt around on the floor and found—the catnip mouse Dora had given her cats.

"What have we here?" Ben squinted as the motion of picking up the mouse caused its belled collar to start tinkling.

"That's—" Arley snatched it from him, grateful he'd dimmed the lights when he'd sat down to watch TV "—just part of an audiovisual demonstration I was planning at the school."

"That little thing? What is it?"

"Nothing important." She struggled to her feet and carelessly tossed the felt mouse over one shoulder, hoping it would land behind the stereo.

"Nothing like casual housekeeping. Will you remember where you put it?" he asked.

"I decided not to use it, after all."

"Then that's a good place for it. Come here." He reached for her again, but she stepped away.

The incident with the mouse had brought her back to reality. The problem remained. Even if she found new homes for Samson and Delilah, the other members of the pet underground would still be in the same predicament. As Dora had said, they were counting on her.

"I thought you wanted coffee," she said.

"I can't remember back that far. Is that what I wanted?"

"Isn't it?"

"If you say so." Back on the couch again but obviously not happy with the way things were going, he took an obedient swallow and choked. "This is really awful."

She sipped her own coffee and grimaced. "I guess I used too much powder."

"I guess you did."

"I'll make more." She started to get up, but he pulled her down again.

"Stay. A cup of coffee I can get anywhere."

Weakening from this fresh assault on her senses, she did as he asked, or more likely, as part of her begged her to.

The tapping at the door didn't register until their lips were a hair's breadth apart.

Ben exhaled through clenched teeth. "Do you plan to answer?"

She didn't have to answer. She knew who it was. She'd told Dora she'd be back around eleven-thirty and she'd collect the kittens. How could she have forgotten?

"Arlene?" came the high, tremulous voice. "Is the coast clear?"

Super. Gesturing for Ben to stay where he was, Arley flew across the room and opened the door just wide enough for Dora to see her face.

"Hi," she said cheerily, rolling her eyes to let Dora know that the coast was definitely not clear. "I have, uh, company."

"You mean *he's* in there?" the woman asked in a stage whisper that seemed louder than any shout. "I thought maybe you'd forgotten. Lovey Bear and Pansy Puss are jealous about—"

"Yes, I can lend you some aspirin," Arley interrupted.

"Aspirin?" the woman echoed.

"Sometimes aspirin helps you sleep. I'm sorry I don't have any sleeping pills."

"I never have trouble sleeping. I don't—" When Dora broke off, her expression showed signs of the proverbial light bulb. "Oh, yes. I understand. An aspirin. Thank you." Deliberately keeping her gaze away from Ben, she stood in the doorway with clasped hands and waited while Arley flew to the bathroom for the pills.

"Good night, then."

The woman leaned closer. "Come over when *he's* gone," she whispered.

Arley stood still for a moment after she'd closed the door, afraid to look at Ben. That had definitely been the last straw. She couldn't lie any longer.

But would he care about the plight of two homeless kittens any more than her father had cared that long-ago day?

"What's bothering you?" Ben asked. "Sometimes talking helps."

She sat on the couch again. This time, though, she perched on the edge. "I was thinking of you, actually."

"If I put that furrow in your lovely brow, I apologize. But what did I do?"

"Oh, it's a mixture of a lot of things, I suppose."

"Name one."

She paused, trying to figure out where to begin. "I still can't help but wonder about your stand on pets."

"That again." He let his head fall back onto the couch.

"You asked me," she reminded him. "And I think caring about something that can't fend for itself says something about a person."

"And I think I'd better go." Slapping his hands against his knees in exasperation, he stood.

She stood, too. "What about the fish?"

"What fish are those?"

"You can tell me it isn't any of my business, but I heard that you refused to rent one of the apartments to a man just because he had a few goldfish."

He was silent for a moment, then started for the door. "You're right. It isn't any of your business. Maybe I'm against computer education. Maybe I think kids should learn that work is work and play is play. Their characters will be a damn sight better for it in the long run."

"I understand," she said, bristling over this unwarranted attack. It didn't help to recognize that their argument wasn't about computers. Several times he'd agreed enthusiastically with her defense of them. He was only using that subject as a counter attack to her charges. "In my line of work, I meet many pigheaded people who can't take criticism."

"You aren't making any sense," he muttered.

"Aren't I? Do dogs leave trash on the pool deck? Do goldfish play loud music all night?"

"If you're talking about Fitzpatrick, I'll admit he isn't an ideal tenant."

"Then why don't you put him against the wall and have him shot?"

"That wouldn't suit you, either, would it? From what I saw the other night, the two of you are pretty chummy."

"I stopped by his apartment after I left you. So?"

"After telling me you had to get home for an important phone call."

"I was only there for a minute. It didn't mean anything."

"I didn't suppose it did. I only wondered."

"Maybe you should put me against that wall, too."

He rubbed the back of his neck. "What are we fighting about? I honestly don't know."

The silence that fell between them seemed endless. Obviously Ben wasn't going to be the first one to speak.

But where could she start? She exhaled deeply in preparation. "Last Saturday," she began, turning her back so that she wouldn't have to look at him, "or was it the Saturday before last?" So many things had happened to her lately, she'd lost track of time.

She didn't get any further. On Jonathan's stereo, Elvis Presley was complaining, at full volume, that he was "all shook up."

"I've had enough," Ben growled. He threw open the door and rushed down the stairs.

Despite the distance, she clearly heard his fist bang heavily on the other man's door. The voices started at a rumble, then got louder.

Quietly, Arley crept out of her room and went partway down the stairs.

"Before you took over, this wasn't a mausoleum," Jonathan was saying, his voice slurred as if he'd had a few drinks.

Ben, probably trying not to disturb the other tenants, spoke too softly to be understood, but from Jonathan's silence, Arley could tell that Ben was making his point.

"Look, Travis, if you have problems with your girl," Jonathan shouted, "don't take it out on me."

"Keep it down. Arley doesn't have anything to do with this."

"Doesn't she?" Jonathan laughed and said something else, which Arley couldn't hear.

Ben's retort was muffled, as well.

"They sure as hell knew what they were doing when they picked her for the job," Jonathan said, louder this time.

"What job is that?" Ben's voice was finally audible.

"Forget it."

"I think you'd better tell me."

"Are you sure you want to hear this?" taunted Jonathan.

"Go on."

The quiet that followed was more ominous than the shouting had been. Arley squeezed her eyes shut, and when she opened them again, the two men had disappeared into the apartment.

The charade was over.

Jonathan was often immature, but he was rarely vicious, so he must have been upset before Ben had started to lecture him. She had a feeling Jonathan wouldn't hold back any secrets. By the time Ben came out of that apartment, he would know everything. She had not only deceived him, but had made a fool out of him in front of his tenants.

Dora had come out of her apartment and was standing at the head of the stairs, twisting her hands. "The jig's up for all of us."

"Do you think he'll throw us out?" Caroline Oates asked from her own doorway.

"I can't talk about it now," Arley said, biting back a sob. She retrieved her kittens and hurried back into her apartment.

CHAPTER EIGHT

THUMP, THUD, SWHOOSH.

The racket had been going on for what seemed like hours, but Arley was so emotionally exhausted, she'd managed to ignore it for a while and drift in and out of sleep.

Finally, in exasperation, she removed Delilah from her lap and set her beside the pillow. Muttering to herself, she got up and crossed to the window to look out.

Ben was on the basketball court—running, faking, dribbling. At this hour? Thump, thud, swhoosh, as the ball dropped through the net and into Ben's waiting hands. Then the whole thing started again.

Obviously Ben wasn't content to simply fill her waking hours with unease, but was also determined to keep her from getting some much-needed sleep. Thump, thud, swhoosh.

The moon had gone behind the clouds, and she couldn't see him clearly. He was only a figure in a colorless sweatshirt and jeans, moving with easy grace. Feeling like a voyeur, she stood for a very long time, hypnotized.

What would he say when they came face-to-face again? More important, what would *she* say?

She had an impulse to shout to him that her cats didn't make noise under windows and keep people awake all night. She had another even stronger urge to call out and ask him to come to her. Would he, if she did? He had been so angry.

Had he continued shooting baskets, she might have stood at the window for the rest of the night. But he gave it up at last and disappeared, leaving her alone, staring at nothing.

The rest of the weekend was quiet. The other tenants were lying low, dreading the aftermath of Friday night's revelations. On Monday, groggy from lack of sleep, Arley anguished over what she should do.

Should she slide a note under Ben's door, accepting all blame, begging him to be merciful to the others and giving notice before he evicted her?

In the end, she decided that would be melodramatic and would accomplish nothing. Better to pack up her possessions and steal away as silently as she could—once she'd found a place to go.

Suzette appeared at her door bright and early, begging a lift to work. Her car she said, was in the shop for servicing. But Arley knew her well enough to decide there was more to it.

"I wanted to talk to you about Jonathan," Suzette said finally, as they waited for a traffic light to change.

"Not now."

"I want to explain why he did what he did. We'd had a terrible fight earlier, he and I. So when Trav came storming over ready to tell him off, Jonathan blew up."

"I don't feel like talking at all," Arley warned her, "and I certainly don't want to talk about that... that..."

"He feels absolutely terrible about what happened."

"He should." Arley tightened her grip on the steering wheel as a yellow Thunderbird with fingers of fire painted on its side streaked in front of her without signaling.

"Jonathan has more of a temper than I realized." A small smile played on Suzette's lips as if she was secretly pleased. "You see, I let it slip that I'd started dating him as a way to make Trav jealous, and he turned purple."

That would do the trick, Arley thought, given how the two men already felt about each other. And it was probably the reason Jonathan had paid her a visit earlier that same night.

"I had no idea he cared so much for me. He finds it difficult to show his feelings, I guess. His ego's very fragile."

"Fragile!" Arley almost choked on the word.

"His parents traveled when he was small, and he was left in the care of an aunt and uncle a lot of the time."

"That's his excuse for deliberately causing people to be evicted?"

"In a way. Don't you consider a miserable childhood extenuating circumstances?"

"Can we forget this for now? I have a lot on my mind."

"They didn't particularly care for children," Suzette went on, as if she hadn't heard. "He thought he had to smile all the time to make them like him."

"Maybe he should try therapy."

"He is, in a manner of speaking." Suzette dug a lipstick out of her handbag, applied it and studied herself in the visor mirror. "I'm acting as his therapist."

"That should be a big help."

"He's been telling me the story of his life, and it's really interesting. Those early days, I think, left him with a need to make every woman he meets fall in love with him."

"If that's true, he's failing miserably." Traffic slowed as a flashing sign indicated that the left lane was closed ahead. Arley slowly applied the brake.

"Hmm. Well, in my opinion, if you can have compassion for animals, you should have some left for him." Suzette put her lipstick away and brought out a small mirrored case that held six different shades of eye shadow. "Is Trav really going to ask Dora and the others to leave?"

"What do you think? He was livid. Jonathan led him to believe we were conspiring to make a fool out of him."

"Weren't you?"

"No. At least I wasn't."

Suzette decided against a new application of eye shadow as the glass-and-steel building that housed the travel agency where she worked loomed into sight. "Poor Jonathan is going to be devastated."

Poor Jonathan? Arley thought as she pulled up to the curb.

Suzette snapped her handbag closed and put the strap over her shoulder. "Have a good day," she sang, as she got out and slammed the car door. "Don't worry about me getting home. I have a ride."

"I wasn't worried," Arley said under her breath.

Contrary to Suzette's parting wish, the day wasn't good at all but long and hectic. It began with Arley discovering that the substitute aide had forgotten to tell her about a teachers' meeting being held—at that moment—in a school auditorium three blocks away.

On her way out, she found a note in her incoming basket saying that the fellow who'd promised to take Rags had changed his mind. He was sorry, but his wife felt that a pet would interfere with their vacations. This, after Arley had called Mildred Barnes and told her she'd found the dog a new home.

"Are you sure?" Mildred had asked. "I can't keep him here much longer."

"Positive. He'll even have a yard."

"Because if you're not one hundred percent sure, I'll have to take him to the shelter this afternoon. The strain of sneaking him in and out is killing me."

"I'm sure. If it doesn't work out, I'll…I'll take him myself."

When she'd blurted out the offer, which was ridiculous under the circumstances, she'd figured it was only a formality. The man had been enthusiastic about the idea. His twelve-year-old son had wanted a dog for years, and was jumping up and down with excitement, he'd said.

Now she had to call Mildred and break the bad news.

"Hi. This is Arley Gordon," she began, when the woman came on the line.

"I knew it," Mildred groaned.

"I'm terribly sorry. The man seemed so sure."

"I know. It isn't your fault. Anyway, I have a possible taker. One of the kids in my sixth-period class is interested. If he can persuade his mom. Keep your fingers crossed."

"I will. And my toes."

To complete her perfect day, just as Arley was going to lunch, she discovered something misfiled in the microfiche drawer. On a hunch, she checked others and discovered that the temporary aide had filed everything by the wrong code numbers. The whole system was botched up.

She'd had to work straight through lunch, and even had to lug some of the drawers home with her to correct the mess. But she didn't mind. Work helped redirect her thoughts.

The streaks of orange that still remained in the deepening violet sky were wispy and few, when, aching with tension, Arley inched into her parking spot.

As she pulled a load of file drawers from her trunk, a change in the sign that hung over the entrance caught her eye. The new wording brought forth tears she'd managed to contain up until that point.

Ben hadn't wasted any time in changing the No Vacancy sign to Vacancy. Was that how he planned to tell her to leave? Did he despise her so much that he didn't even want to look her in the eye when he evicted her?

As usual, he was working at his open window, but as she also could have predicted, he didn't glance up.

Overcome by several nameless emotions, she dried her eyes, approached his door, and knocked.

"I'm working," she heard him call.

"I realize you're anxious to see the last of me," she told the closed door. "But you might have been gentlemanly enough to wait until I'm gone before you start advertising the availability of my apartment."

The door swung open and hit the wall with a thump. Ben's dark hair was disheveled and his face was shadowed with stubble. He wore a rumpled shirt with paint streaks across the stomach and jeans with a tear at the knee. "What are you talking about?"

"The Vacancy sign." Her voice broke and she had to clear her throat.

"A vacant apartment is money lost." He yanked off his glasses and set them on the table beside him.

"I hope you'll give the others time to find new places. It's going to be difficult for those on fixed incomes."

He gave her a devastating glare. "I can't believe you're saying this to me, Arley. What kind of a monster do you think I am?"

"I don't know. How many kinds are there?"

He turned away, then turned back again, shaking his head in disbelief. "We've spent hours together. Hours I considered special. I thought I knew you as well as I could ever know anybody. I thought you knew me."

She'd thought so, too. "I suppose you didn't hang that Vacancy sign."

"The vacancy is for Hal Nordoff's apartment. He's retiring at the end of the month and moving back to Poplar Bluff. I told you that."

"Oh." Had he? Arley heard Ben's answer, yet it didn't really sink in. She was thinking about the sign in front of the building.

Something registered that hadn't registered as she'd stormed past. The No Vacancy sign hadn't been the only one replaced, had it?

She concentrated, trying to picture the sign again, hoping she was right. Belatedly, the rest of the wording zoomed through her mind. Could it be?

With Ben loping along behind her, she hurried back to the entrance. *Yes.* The No Pets sign had been taken down. In its place was one that read Small Pets Considered.

"Oh, Ben!" she cried, throwing her arms out in exhilaration. Unaware that he was only inches behind her, she whirled and slammed into him. "Do you mean it about the pets?"

"After that argument with Fitzpatrick Friday, I decided I might as well have everything out in the open." He put his hands on her shoulders to help her regain her balance, then let them drop to his sides quickly, as if he didn't want her to get the wrong idea. "It's been as much of a strain on me as it's been on the rest of you."

"What do you mean?" His words seemed to echo in her mind. "What do you mean, it's been a strain on you?"

His laugh was cynical, and he gestured toward the breezeway. "Climb a ladder sometime, Arley. Look down. Tell me what you see."

"Ladder?" she repeated, still not understanding.

"The day you brought your furry roommates home in that cardboard box. How could you imagine I'd miss them from where I was standing?"

"You saw them? But why did you...?" Words failed her.

"If it's any consolation, the others were even more obvious. Dora tucking the cats into her bag—ears and tails sticking out and all those wails of protest. Ebert engaging me in conversation about the stock market while his wife tip-toes past. Caroline Oates calling me into her apartment about nonexistent repairs. Once it was something about a bathroom mirror that needed to be re-silvered. I had to give an award-winning performance to pull it off."

"You knew all along," she said dully.

"I decided that if everyone thought I wasn't aware of their pets, they'd be more discreet. I didn't want dogs barking at six o'clock in the morning and cats using the flower beds for a litter box."

"And you let us go on..."

"It seemed like a good idea."

Dazed, Arley allowed herself to remember the heart-stopping events of the days that followed her finding Samson and Delilah. Part of her wanted to accuse him of being insensitive by letting everyone worry unnecessarily. Another part wanted to kiss him and tell him how wonderful he was.

Judging by the combative way they stood, though, she wouldn't do either.

"May I tell the others the good news?" she said quietly.

"I think they already know." He jerked his head toward the landing, where a gleeful Dora was hugging Edna Ebert while a beaming Caroline Oates stood nearby.

"What about Jonathan? Are you asking him to leave?" Arley asked, remembering Suzette's concern.

"I was looking forward to giving him notice. The man doesn't know the meaning of the word 'courtesy.' But when he actually came over this morning to apologize and speak on behalf of the building's pet population, I was too astounded to do it."

"Jonathan apologized?" Arley couldn't imagine the insurance man lowering himself enough for that. Suzette's therapy must have been working.

"He promised to keep the music down. While I'm not sure I believe him, it'll be a lot easier for me to give him another chance than to paint and recarpet his apartment. His idea of a color scheme is frightening."

At least Suzette would be pleased. Poor, dear Jonathan wouldn't be displaced. "I'm glad," Arley said, meaning it—though she didn't know why.

"That's right." Ben bent over to yank out a gangly weed that had somehow escaped his notice before. It was an action taken, she decided, to help him avoid eye contact. "You owe him a debt of gratitude, don't you?"

"Why is that?"

"Thanks to him, everything's out in the open. You don't have to stand for any more basketball lessons or bad spaghetti dinners. You don't have to go on pretending."

"I wasn't pretending."

"You didn't accept my dinner invitation only to throw me off the scent?"

"Maybe at first. But then—"

"You didn't agree to play basketball only to get me away from the window? And what about those sudden impulses you had to put your arms around me? Weren't they carefully planned tactics to keep me in line?"

A wave of misery swept through her, and she knotted her hands together to keep her feelings from showing. "You can't think everything was an act."

"Can't I? Lord knows, I tried hard enough to get you to tell me what was going on."

Yes, he had, she realized now. "All those silly sayings you kept spouting. The cat's out of the bag. Has the cat got your tongue?"

"A few hints to give you a push toward confiding in me."

"I wondered," she said, remembering. Even the movie he'd suggested their seeing—*The Curse of the Cat People.*

The automatic sprinkler system sputtered, gave a warning spray, then went on in earnest, wetting Ben's jeans up to the knees. His only reaction was to step to one side.

"You know what I hated most?" He pulled his lips into a straight, hard line.

"No."

The sky had darkened to a murky purple. The heat of day still remained, but there was a cool breeze that rippled over her skin, making her shiver.

"The part about you, one of the cowering little mice, being elected to hang a bell around my neck and sound the alarm for the others."

A defensive remark rose inside her—something that would explain how bad policies made by unfeeling landlords forced people to take drastic steps—but she bit it back.

"I want to thank you, anyway," she began, "On behalf of—"

"Spare me the speech." He thrust out one hand, as if it held a cross and Arley was Countess Dracula. "I have a deadline to meet. If you'll excuse me."

CHAPTER NINE

WHAT BEN HAD SAID about the mice playing while the cat was away was doubly true at their apartment building. The news that he would be away for a few days spread quickly. Though his new policy openly declared that pets were welcome, an air of disbelief remained, as if the privilege were a cruel joke and could, at any given moment, be yanked away.

Everyone with pets took advantage of Ben's absence. Cats were allowed to sun under their owners' supervision. Dogs were exercised. Dora even brought out collars and leashes to stake Pansy Puss and Lovey Bear in a small area of the grassy yard near the trash bins.

"Maybe when you've won Mr. Travis over completely, Arley, he'll agree to turn this part of the yard into a play area for our pets."

"I wouldn't count on it," Arley warned, thinking about the fragility of her current relationship with Ben.

"I'll bet he'll be eating out of your hand in another month."

"Please. Don't even think it," Arley begged, wanting no more rumors like that to start. Inevitably, they'd come back to haunt her.

Sleep was elusive during the nights Ben was absent. She missed him much more than she would have if all had been right between them. Had they parted on friendly terms, she might have contented herself with reliving moments they'd shared and making plans for more. As things stood, there was nothing for her to look forward to upon his return, but regret.

Invariably she woke at four in the morning when, as regular as clockwork, footsteps sounded past her door. Mr. Ebert worked nights and always got home about that time. He likely made no more noise than he always had, but recently, she'd been sleepless enough to notice.

By the time Ben returned on Thursday, she'd written and rewritten a dozen possible scenarios in her mind. Scenarios designed to explain to him why she'd behaved as she had. Though she always tried to be optimistic, most of them ended unhappily.

Now he sat at his drawing table, stern-looking in his reading glasses, apparently too engrossed in whatever he was doing to notice when she passed. How much time could it take to wave, or to step over to the door and say hi? She didn't expect him to suggest they take up where they'd left off before all the trouble started, but they could at least be civil, couldn't they?

"Ben's always preoccupied when he's working," Suzette assured her when Arley thought she would burst if she didn't talk about her unhappiness with someone. "If he's finishing up an assignment, he wouldn't notice an eight-point-one earthquake. That's one thing about Jonathan—when he's with a woman, he pays complete attention to her. Did I tell you he's a wonderful dancer?"

"Only a few dozen times." Although Suzette's interest in Jonathan had begun as a ploy to set a spark to Ben, it had become something more. Maybe it was her influence that caused Jonathan to keep his promise not to crank up the volume of his stereo. Arley still didn't like him, but she had to give him credit.

"I know he has faults," said Suzette. "But they're understandable, don't you think, considering his background? Besides, I'm working on them."

"You can't alter a man's basic personality as you would a dress that doesn't fit properly," Arley felt it necessary to remind her friend.

Suzette tossed her head. "Twiddle-de-dee, aren't we philosophical today? Speaking of that, Trav could benefit from a bit of alteration."

Arley wasn't planning to argue. She thought it ironic, though, now that her friend had shifted her interests to Jonathan, giving her a clear field with Ben, it didn't do her any good. "I suppose we all could."

Saturday was an especially difficult day. As usual, Ben was working in the yard taking care of the chores that had piled up during the week. So much time had passed since they'd spoken that Arley no longer wanted a confrontation. Perhaps, she decided, it was better for them to keep away from each other and let any ill feelings die a gradual death.

From experience, she'd learned that Ben moved fast and might be anywhere. With that in mind, she'd stayed in her apartment, working on a project that had been discussed at several PTA meetings.

By Sunday, feeling strongly the effects of her self-imposed confinement, she decided to spend some time sprucing up her apartment and adding a few touches that showed the new carpet to advantage.

Better that, than dragging herself around, filled with self-pity.

To start, she dug into her cedar chest and brought out the treasured needlepoint pillows her grandmother had left her. Done in shades of pink and rose, they complemented the new flooring perfectly.

She was humming to herself as she came back from the trash area, thinking about buying the small mirrored case she'd seen in a store window. It was expensive, but would be just the thing to display the delicate little glass animals her grandmother had given to her, as well. Maybe Ben wouldn't object to them, she thought wryly. They didn't bark, serenade the moon or dig holes in his precious geranium bed.

She'd paused at the side of the building and was using the hose to rinse down the sides of her trash basket, when she caught sight of a pretty black woman in a yellow cotton shirt and white jeans coming up the front steps.

The visitor stood for a moment, looking around, then dug into her handbag.

Ben, who'd seen her, too, appeared in the breezeway. He wiped his hands on a rag he had stuffed in his belt and headed toward her. "Can I help you?"

"I hope I'm at the right place. I'm Mildred Barnes, a teacher from Fairfax High. I'm looking for Arlene—" She broke off and smiled. "I've forgotten her last name. It's on a card here in my bag."

Mildred Barnes. Omigosh. Arley hadn't recognized her at first. Oh, Lord, probably the woman hadn't been able to find a home for Rags and now was here to see if Arley would keep her promise to look after the dog herself.

To Ben, Small Pets Considered probably didn't mean two cats and a dog.

"We have an Arlene Gordon," he was saying. "Just up those steps and to your—"

"*Ben!*" Arley shrieked. Dropping her waste-basket, she burst through the breezeway at a run. "Come here. Hurry!"

"Just a minute," he called back.

"Please come now. *Please!*"

"Go ahead. It seems you have an emergency," the other woman said.

Arley clasped her hands together in mock—or maybe not so mock—anguish. "A spider," she said, as Ben joined her. "A huge, black, hairy spider!"

"Since when are you afraid of spiders?"

"This one could be a black widow." She pointed.

He looked over his shoulder at Mildred, probably trying to decide if he should finish with her first.

"I was taking out my garbage and it . . . it sprang at me," Arley gasped, hurling herself against him.

"A spider sprang?"

"I'm not sure what it was. It was crawly and terrible." She pressed her face against his chest and whimpered.

"The beast that ate St. Louis?"

"Don't joke about it. Go see for yourself."

His arms had gone around her automatically and his lips brushed her hair. "It's okay," he said softly, his hands gently stroking her back. "You'll have to show me where."

"I can't. It crawled under the big bin. You'd better take something to fight it off."

"I think I can handle it," he said, shaking his head as he went in the direction she indicated. "If I'm not back in five minutes, call out a SWAT team."

"Mildred," she said in a hoarse whisper when he was out of sight. She touched a hand to the woman's elbow and led her toward the sidewalk. "Let's talk someplace else."

"Was there really a black widow?"

"Yes, no. Where's Rags?"

"There's trouble." Mildred allowed herself to be steered down the steps and to the right of the building, where they'd be out of Ben's earshot. "Rags has been found out. Somebody heard him and turned us in."

"Oh, no."

"Oh, yes. And the timing is terrible. Remember the student I told you about? His mother said they might be able to take the dog on a trial basis. But they have to check with the building manager."

That didn't sound too promising.

"Can you keep Rags that long?"

"No way. The dog goes or I do, my dear landlord says." The woman shrugged. "I wanted to talk to you first. I really have no choice. He has to go to the animal shelter."

Visions of the poor little dog who'd already been cruelly abandoned once swept through Arley's mind.

"Don't do that," she said, not wanting to think about what she was saying. "Bring him here. I'll take him until you hear from that woman and her son."

"Oh, can you?"

"No, but I will. You'll have to keep him until to-morrow morning, though. That'll give me a chance to talk to my own landlord."

The woman frowned. "Maybe I can—I don't know—pretend to be struck down with the twenty-four-hour Bavarian flu."

"Is there such a thing?"

The woman fluttered one hand. "There is now."

"Good." Arley glanced over her shoulder. If Ben had returned, she couldn't see him from here. "To-morrow morning at six, park in the alley behind my building. I'll be there waiting."

"Bless you." Mildred gave Arley's hand a grateful squeeze. "Rags looked so sad this morning I swear he knew something was up."

"I didn't see anything," Ben said when he came back just seconds after Arley had returned to where she'd been standing before she'd sent him on his mission.

"Maybe I was wrong," she said, her relief at her success giving her voice a slight tremor.

"Let's hope so." He wore the unperturbed expression of a man who'd grown to expect just about any-thing from her. "But I'm curious. Don't spiders rate the same loving care you give other critters? Don't they have feelings, too?"

"You're right," she admitted, although she knew he was joking. "They really are remarkable, when you think about it. Those intricate webs. Have you ever watched a spider making one?"

"Not that I can remember."

"I—I don't know why I reacted like that."

"Maybe you've been working too hard," he suggested.

"Maybe," she agreed, avoiding his eyes.

"The woman who was here." Ben glanced around. "I think she was looking for you."

"She's gone," someone said.

In her panic, Arley hadn't noticed Jonathan lying on one of the deck chairs around the pool. His amusement was apparent. "She said she thought she'd come to the wrong place. The building she wanted was on the next street."

Arley didn't dare look at Jonathan. "Thank you, anyway, for coming to my rescue," she told Ben. "Even though, as it turned out, I didn't need rescuing."

"Anytime." He seemed to be holding back a grin. "I'd appreciate it if you didn't spread your story about the spider around. Some of the tenants might be afraid to take out their garbage."

"I won't," she promised, the heat of embarrassment spreading through her from forehead to toes. He hadn't been fooled by her supposed fear of spiders. He'd assumed, as anyone would under the circumstances, that she'd invented the whole story just to talk to him again.

Only when he'd gone, did she let herself glance at Jonathan. When she did, he raised his beer can in a salute. "Nice going," he said, donning a knowing grin.

That did it.

Even if it meant sleeping in her car for the next month, complete with litter box and cat toys, she promised herself no more lies. And it was a promise she would keep. Starting now.

FEELING SOMETHING OF WHAT Marie Antoinette must have felt as she walked to the guillotine, Arley followed the sound of hammering to the laundry room, where Ben was fixing a sagging cabinet door. The back of his forest-green shirt was damp with perspiration, and his hair stood on end because he'd run his hand through it. He must have heard her approach, but he didn't react.

"There wasn't any spider," she said when he set the hammer down and picked up a screwdriver.

He didn't answer.

"I made it up to get you out of the way."

He still didn't say anything.

"Mildred Barnes was looking for me. She has a dog who's been horribly abused. His name is Rags, and she can't keep him."

To her dismay, as she tried to convey the hopelessness of Rags's plight, she discovered that all the skills she'd acquired in her public-speaking classes were gone. She was aware that she was explaining things badly. Still, she rattled on faster and faster, like a train running downhill with no one at the throttle.

"You already have two cats," Ben reminded her. The words came out as if they'd been forced through clenched teeth. "Isn't that enough?"

"I'll only have the dog for a few days," she said. "A home will be opening up for him then."

She hoped.

"You want to take in a dog you don't know, when you've just had new carpet installed? How do you know he's housebroken?"

"Oh, he is. He's sweet and gentle and perfectly trained."

"Three animals in a one-bedroom apartment?"

"The city allows three."

"The city doesn't own this place." He put the screwdriver back in his toolbox and selected another, larger one. "Dammit, Arley, you're pushing me too far. You're taking advantage of our relationship."

Relationship? What relationship, she wondered miserably. Why didn't he turn around and look at her? Talking to his back was unsettling. "If you won't let me keep him here, they'll put him to sleep."

All of a sudden she was ten years old again and her father was lecturing her about the impossibility of taking in the stray pup. Arley could hear the screeching of the car wheels and the terrible thud. She felt like crying, but she wouldn't. Not now.

"He's just a little dog," she went on. "You won't even know he's around."

Ben exchanged the screwdriver for the hammer again. Choosing a nail from one of the plastic compartments in his toolbox, he held it in place, raised the hammer and brought it down—onto his thumb. With a yelp of pain, he let the hammer slide down his knees to the cement floor.

"Are you all right?" Concerned, Arley took a step toward him.

"It's okay," he muttered around the injured thumb he'd put in his mouth.

"The people who owned the dog before aban-doned him without food or water," she began again, when he'd recuperated enough to pick up the ham-mer. "He nearly died."

"I said, it's okay." Ben's voice was charged with impatience.

"You mean...it's okay about Rags? I can bring him here?"

"That's what I said." He patted a hand along the floor, searching for the nail he'd dropped. He found it, saw it was too bent to use and tossed it into a waste container in the corner.

"I promise to pay for any damage. Not that there'll be any. He's—"

"Perfectly trained, I know," he parroted.

"I told Mildred to bring him over tomorrow."

Ben's laugh was without mirth. "You told her that already? Without checking with me?"

"Yes," she admitted. "But I'm checking with you now."

"After you made the arrangements."

"He'll only be here a few days."

"I told you it was all right," he said sharply. "Can I get on with this?"

"Thank you," she murmured.

As she moved away, he was rummaging through his toolbox again, muttering to himself about charging admission to allow people admittance to the zoo.

CHAPTER TEN

"YOU'VE GOT ANTS," Suzette said, appearing from nowhere as Arley came up the stairs and pointing at the floor.

"That's all I need." Arley looked at the trail of insects moving through the crack at the hinged side of the door, over the threshold and into the kitchen.

Somehow, Samson had managed to paw open one of the cabinets. That done, he'd found the bag of kitten kibble and had torn a hole in the side. The meaty little pellets were scattered all over the kitchen floor, providing an unexpected feast for the six-legged invaders. Apparently having eaten his fill, the kitten was now curled up with Delilah on the mat in front of the sink.

"Isn't it amazing how smart these little creepy crawlies are?" Suzette said.

"Amazing," Arley groaned.

"In this hot weather, it doesn't take much to attract them. I put everything in airtight containers."

"That's what I should have done." Arley shook her head at the mess.

"Oh, the joys of parenthood. You're lucky Trav didn't track the trail to your door. Or maybe you don't care now that he knows about the pet underground."

"He'd probably count each ant as a pet," Arley said grimly, regretting the words the minute she said them. They were unfair. Under the circumstances, Ben had been very reasonable.

She stood for a moment, hands on hips. She'd have to get the bag of kibble to the trash before the ants found other goodies to raid, but she didn't want to pass Ben again. He might change his mind about Rags if he was aware of the mess.

Suzette opened the refrigerator, took out a diet cola and ripped off the metal tab. "Men!" she snarled, going back to the living room to drop onto the couch with her legs outstretched.

Amazed by her friend's negative tone at the mention of her favorite subject and the ungraceful posture she'd adopted, Arley noticed something else, too. Suzette looked unlike herself. She wasn't wearing any makeup and her hair was straggly. She was wearing a simple striped T-shirt and jeans.

"Are you all right?"

"No. I'm sick." She slouched still more. "Sick of Jonathan."

Arley had been expecting this. Suzette's romances never lasted long, and this unlikely one should have been over more quickly than most. "You had a quarrel?"

"Not exactly." Suzette studied her fingernails. "Who was that guy back in the early eighteen hundreds who took six hours to dress every day? He had a wardrobe full of fancy suits he didn't pay for, with lace at the collar and cuffs?"

"Beau Brummell?"

Suzette snapped her fingers. "That's him. I'd bet a hundred bucks that Jonathan is Beau Brummell reincarnated."

"What did he do?"

"He didn't do anything. He's just behaving like Jonathan. And I'm through with him."

Arley opened the cabinet under the sink and brought out a large, brown paper bag. Picking up the kibble bag by the corner, she deposited it carefully in the brown one.

As Arley swept the kibble-covered floor, Suzette told her about the party she'd gone to the night before. She'd been bragging about Jonathan to her co-workers for days. He was so handsome. So charming. So...everything. Then she made the mistake of inviting him to attend a barbecue celebrating a friend's fifth wedding anniversary.

"All the other women were talking about how cute he was," Suzette said. "At first."

"But?"

"But the guys were doing the cooking and started fooling around, you know, and some barbecue sauce spattered down the front of Jonathan's shirt. Instead of laughing with the others, he started hollering about how that was his favorite shirt and how much it cost. Everybody had suggestions for taking out the stains. But when they tried to help, he said they were only making things worse."

"I suppose it was embarrassing."

"And that's not all. Later, the guys had a little too much beer and got even more playful. They started pushing each other into the pool, and Jonathan got caught in the middle."

"He ended up in the water?"

Suzette nodded. "But rather than being a good sport, he screamed about how his Italian-made shoes were ruined. We fought all the way home. I've never seen anybody so...so vain."

Unless it was Suzette herself, Arley added silently. "We all have faults," she reminded Suzette, as she sprinkled talcum powder along the trail, hoping to discourage other ants from joining the parade. "I have to take this out now."

Suzette wasn't listening. "I told him I didn't need anybody in my life who didn't know how to have fun."

"What did he say?"

"He called my friends slobs." Her lower lip started to quiver. "Isn't that the same thing as calling me a slob?"

"People say things," Arley soothed, wanting to get outside with the sack before any wily escapees made it to her elbow.

"You were completely right, and I told Jonathan that."

"What do I have to do with this?" Arley wished people wouldn't attribute their own opinions to her.

"You said it doesn't really matter what happened in a person's childhood. It only matters that he is what he is."

"How could I say that when I don't even know what you're talking about?"

"Think of spending your life with somebody who's afraid to get his shoes wet. Somebody who preens in front of a mirror more than you do?"

Spending her life? Arley wondered. Had it come to that? "I'd never thought about it."

"You wouldn't. Trav goes to the other extreme. I mean, sometimes it's hard to tell what color his shirt once was, from all the paint on it." Suzette's sigh trembled as it reached her lips and ended with a sob. She plucked a tissue out of its box and dabbed at her eyes. "Men!"

FORTUNATELY BEN HAD finished whatever he'd been doing in the laundry room. It was empty when Arley passed. That was good. She needed time to think about the events of the past hour.

As she raised the hinged cover of the trash bin, Jonathan appeared beside her with a bag of his own.

"I imagine Suzette explained about the other night," he began. "I'm sorry about blowing the whistle on everybody. But she really knows how to push my buttons. Guess I lost my head. But, hey, everything turned out all right, didn't it?"

"Everything's fine."

He chewed on his bottom lip. "So she's upstairs crying on your shoulder?"

"Don't put me in the middle of this." Arley allowed him to hold open the lid while she dropped her bag into the cavernous bin.

Something about the way he gripped his bag of trash made her wonder if it was only a prop he'd carried as an excuse to talk to her about Suzette. She began to walk away.

"I don't understand that woman." He let the lid bang closed and rushed after Arley. "I assumed she wanted me to make an impression on her friends. So I tried to do that. I even had my car waxed. You'd have thought I violated some tribal custom, from the way she acted.''

"Maybe she wanted you to get into the spirit of things.''

"The spirit of things? By behaving like a Neanderthal? By splashing around in a swimming pool in my best sport coat and a pair of new shoes? When I told her how much those shoes cost, she only got more upset with me.''

"She probably would have preferred to see you wear something a bit more casual to a barbecue.''

"Hell, she knows I'm not the type to wear cutoffs and T-shirts. Anyway, she didn't tell me it was a barbecue. Those people may be friends of hers, but they're . . .''

"Slobs?'' Arley finished for him.

"She told you what I said? I didn't call *her* a slob.'' He gestured helplessly. "I mean, who would? She's anything but.''

"Tell her.''

"She's beautiful. I'd put her up against anybody, and she'd come out the winner.''

"*Tell* her.''

"I tried.'' Jonathan looked defeated. "She won't talk to me.''

Arley actually felt sorry for him. "Try again,'' she said. "What have you got to lose?''

"Why should I be the one to apologize?'' he called after her as she reached the top of the stairs. This time his voice was loud, as if he was hoping Suzette would hear him.

His theatrics were wasted. Suzette had left Arley's apartment and she was alone for the first time since her words with Ben.

Giving in to the weariness caused by all the emotions she'd experienced lately, she sank into a chair and closed her eyes, trying to summon the strength she needed to get through the rest of the day. Tomorrow would have to take care of itself.

Enough, she thought, as a small hiss, followed by a low growl, reminded her she wasn't alone at all. Samson was arching his back, stalking a plastic wrapper that had fallen out of the garbage can.

Moping would do no good. Her rapidly growing family had to eat. It was possible that Mildred would forget to bring food when she arrived with Rags the next morning, and Arley would have to buy kibble for dogs, as well as cats. This time she'd put it in a plastic container with an airtight, Samson-proof lid.

Shopping list in hand and still feeling unsettled, she didn't notice Ben in the supermarket produce section, frowning over a basket of strawberries, until it was too late to retreat. He'd changed into a ginger-colored shirt that made his eyes look like brown sugar. The sleeves were rolled up, reminding her of the strength she'd felt in his arms, and his collar was open, allowing her a glimpse of the dark curling hair on his chest.

In his concentration, his hair had flopped down over his forehead, giving him an innocent, carefree look that made all her antagonism, if any remained, evaporate.

"You don't give up, do you?" he asked, his smile of greeting disappearing so quickly she wasn't sure its presence hadn't been just wishful thinking.

She steadied herself for round two. "What do you mean?"

"All those animal-cruelty brochures and booklets you left in my mailbox. I already told you that dog could stay."

This sounded like Dora's handiwork, Arley thought. "What makes you think I'm guilty?" she asked, although she knew it was absurd considering the time they'd spent talking about the subject.

He tapped a finger against his forehead. "ESP."

She laughed and changed the subject. "I've been meaning to ask you—how was your trip?"

"Trip?"

"The lakefront property you went to see last week."

"Oh, yes. That. Well, it was about what I expected. Lots of water." He studied the carton of strawberries as if it had directions on the side. "You've been busy lately," he said, changing the subject himself.

"It's that time of year. School activities are at their peak." She managed a weak smile, feeling uncomfortable with this oh-so-polite conversation. "How about you?"

"I've run into a few snags with my assignment. I have to do a lot of research. I might start working at the medical center, after all."

Could things be any clearer? He was backing off from her gracefully, wanting to explain why he wouldn't be extending any more invitations—either to dinner or to accompany him on trips to lakefront properties.

"Fewer distractions," she said.

He exchanged the carton of strawberries he'd been holding for another, then looked at her with a curious expression that seemed to say berries were the furthest thing from his mind.

She feigned interest in the strawberries, too. "This is a good price. I should get some."

His lower lip slid forward as he gazed at her. "You never fuss with your hair, do you? You just yank it back and let it do what it will. And as usual you're wearing pants."

Given the current state of their relationship, Arley wasn't sure what to make of his statement. She shrugged. "They're more practical than a skirt."

"Baggy pants, at that. They don't hug you anywhere. I can't even claim you're dressing to attract me, can I?" His smile was tight.

"I'm sorry if you don't like my choice of clothing."

"I didn't say I didn't like it—on you. I'm saying it's deceptive. The kind of thing that catches hold of a man without warning." He grinned. "Take Cleopatra, for example. With her slinky outfits, a man knew right away that he was in trouble. Then there was Scarlett O'Hara, with her hoop skirts and parasols."

No comment she could think of seemed suitable. Instead, she looked down at her hands.

"Pardon me." A heavyset woman in an orange muumuu glared as she pushed her cart between them. "I'd like to have some of those strawberries, too, if you don't mind."

"If you're finished here, why don't you move on?" another woman asked, waiting for Ben to step aside. "Some people come here to shop."

"We're holding up traffic," Ben said, then smiled.

"I'm afraid so."

He really did have wonderful eyes, she thought. She could almost get lost in them. Ben broke their eye contact and looked down at her basket. Swiftly, she shifted her purse to cover the bag of kibble, then laughed at herself, embarrassed. There was no longer any need for secrecy. Not missing the movement, Ben laughed, too.

"I'd better get back," he said. "I might get some work done before I lose the light."

"Good idea," she agreed.

As he started away, he bumped into the woman in the muumuu, causing her to drop her purse. Apologizing profusely, he bent to retrieve it for her. Not waiting to hear the woman express her indignation, Arley quickly maneuvered her cart down the next aisle and out of earshot.

With a relieved sigh, she realized the angry feelings between the two of them had evaporated. Landlord and tenant had spoken pleasantly about nothing important. Things were back to the way they had been before Samson and Delilah had come into her life, and painful as it might have been for Arley, it would make any future meetings between them much more comfortable.

Now was the time to put her regrets aside and concentrate on the problems of the moment. She'd never had a dog before. As she found herself in the pet-food aisle again, she wondered if Rags would like the brand of kibble she'd chosen. Another woman, who appeared to be an old hand at this, was stacking her cart with dozens of cans and economy-size bags. Arley stopped to ask her advice before going to the next aisle for coffee.

Deciding to abandon her cart inside, instead of having to bring it back to the service area after unloading, she had both her arms full when she left the store. She headed in the direction of her car, which in the almost full parking lot wasn't easy to spot. Suddenly she stopped walking. Ahead of her she saw Ben. Though he'd left a good ten minutes before, he was standing beside her car, apparently waiting for her.

"I forgot to ask you," he said when she reached him and he relieved her of the larger of the two bags. "How about our date?"

She swallowed. "I didn't know we had one."

"You promised to let me paint you."

"Oh, that." It seemed so long ago.

"Come on, Arley. You're going to have to meet me halfway on this reconciliation thing if it's going to work."

"Is that what this is?"

"I hope so." Taking her car keys, he opened the door and deposited one sack on the floor and the other on the passenger seat. Then he stood aside so that Arley could get in.

"After this afternoon, I thought you'd want to see me as little as possible," she said.

"That's where you're wrong. I admit I was angry— or maybe hurt—that you didn't feel you could trust me."

"Or maybe both?" she suggested.

"After I thought about it, I realized that you did what you thought you had to do."

"I hated lying to you." She bit her lower lip to control its tremble.

"Understandable." His expression was impish. "You had to wait—and see which way the cat jumped."

"It could have been a *cat*astrophe," she added, warmed by his smile.

"Anyway, you came forward in the end. That's what counts. It was very touching." He picked up her hand and caressed it. "Are we still friends?"

"Still friends," she said, barely able to contain the joy that threatened to overtake her.

"The spider sprang." He chuckled. "That's a gem."

She felt herself blush. "Don't remind me."

"You're right. Let's start over."

"Let's."

She thought for a moment. Today had been beautiful, but she'd only just noticed. The sun was gentle, and the air smelled lush with summer. The sky was a storybook blue, laced only here and there with clouds. She had no reason to believe tomorrow wouldn't bring more of the same weather, and since she had the day off, a picnic lunch in the park would be wonderful. But she wouldn't tell Ben her plan yet. She wanted it to be a surprise.

"I owe you a meal," she said. "How about tomorrow?"

"You're asking me for a date?"

"I am."

"Maybe I should play hard to get."

"Will you?"

"No. You might change your mind. Tomorrow it is. Want me to bring anything? How about wine?"

"No. I'll handle everything."

"That takes care of tomorrow. But it doesn't let you off the hook tonight. You promised to pose for me."

"I said sometime."

He looked at his watch. "Sometime is now. As soon as you get home."

"I've been cleaning," she protested. "I have to shower and change."

"Okay. But don't take time to eat. I'll throw something together. That way we can get down to work. Oh, and wear your hair loose. I like it that way. It'll make for a better composition."

"All right," she agreed, though she preferred pinning it away from her face.

"And to be honest," he went on, "I prefer dresses."

"I understand." She nodded gravely, biting back a smile. "But I'd rather you didn't wear one when you're with me."

He laughed and leaned down to give her a swift, but stunning kiss that made her glad she was already sitting.

"See you later."

Later.

The short and simple word filled her with anticipation. After all the days, hours and minutes of denying herself Ben's company, it was wonderful knowing that, before long, they'd be together again. Really together. That everything would be the way it was before. Except that this time, it would be better. There'd be no secrets between them.

CHAPTER ELEVEN

"I HAVE SOMETHING for you," Arley said. As Ben opened the door to her, she held out a beret she'd found among a jumble of things she'd been gathering to give the local thrift shop. Eric had worn it to a Mardi Gras party they'd attended. A party that had ended badly, as almost everything with him had during their final weeks together. "I thought it might help set a more creative atmosphere."

"Thank you, *madamoiselle*." He plopped it crookedly on his head.

She surveyed the result. "What you need now is a smock. With paint splotches all over it."

"No smocks, unfortunately. But I have a drawer full of shirts, complete with paint splotches."

"That'll do." She sniffed. "I don't smell anything cooking."

"And why would you? Food has no meaning. An artist must be hungry to do his best work. That goes for his model, too."

"You promised me dinner," she said, her hands on her hips.

"We'll send out for pizza when we're through. Lots of cheese. Mushrooms. Green peppers."

She laughed at the terrible French accent he'd assumed and the comical appearance the beret gave him. "And black olives?"

"But of course."

"It doesn't bother you a mite that pizza is Italian, not French?"

"Would you rather I sent out for escargot?"

"No, thanks. I'll settle for the pizza."

After kissing the tip of her nose, he led her to a bar stool he'd set against the wall and covered with a green scarf.

"The couch would be more comfortable," she said when she sat down.

"No comments. You aren't a person. You're an object."

"I see."

"Now for the master's touch." Over her protests, he brought out a comb, gave her a severe center part and smoothed her hair straight to her shoulders.

"I don't like my hair this way."

"Shh." He made an impatient clicking sound with his tongue. "Who's the artist here?"

"I'll answer that when I see the finished product."

"An artist sees light and shadow. He sees curves and angles. I won't see a naked woman when I look at you," he teased, stepping back to study her.

"I guarantee it," she declared. "Because I'll be fully clothed."

"What kind of cooperation is that?" Ben pretended to sulk. "Where would the world be if Mona Lisa had been stubborn with Leonardo?"

"She probably was. Mona Lisa was wearing clothes."

In deference to Ben's wishes, instead of pants, she'd worn a long print skirt of green, lemon and coral with a mint-green blouse of silky crepe. After voicing his approval of the outfit, Ben removed the horseshoe pin she'd placed at the neck of her blouse and added a cameo he'd taken from a lacquered box on the table next to his drawing board.

"This is flea-market finery," he said. "But the effect is right."

"What effect is that?"

"The effect I'm looking for." He turned his head to one side, then the other.

"Can we get on with this?" she said, confident that all the staging was only for fun and that the finished product would be similar to the other illustrations she'd seen. Her likeness would simply be squiggly red and blue lines—her, minus her skin. "I'll give you half an hour. Then we send for pizza."

"An artist can't be expected to punch a time clock."

"A cook can't, either," she said. "In a sense, a cook is also an artist. I plan to make potato salad for tomorrow."

"Didn't your mother ever tell you that potato salad comes in cartons with plastic covers and is found in the deli section of the supermarket?"

"The kind I make involves allowing the potatoes to chill before I go to work on them, and then they have to marinate overnight."

"I'm hungry already," he said.

"Me, too. So let's get a move on here.

"You're a flea-market addict?" she asked, remembering what he'd said a moment before. "I am, too. I buy all sorts of things on impulse, then end up donating them to a friend who takes them to sell at another flea market."

"Hush!" He waved away her commment with mock impatience. "You've broken my concentration, so I'll need an extra half hour."

"It was only worth an extra ten."

"Fifteen."

At last she was correctly posed. A floor lamp had been placed behind her and two table lamps had been set beside her. Chopin was on the turntable—Ben was evidently a holdout against CDs—and Ben stood in front of his drawing board, looking at her through narrowed eyes.

Ordering her to keep perfectly still, he circled, studying her from this angle and that, making her feel as self-conscious as she would have if she weren't wearing any clothes.

But she called on her patience and did as he asked, until finally she couldn't help but notice that his pastel hadn't touched the paper.

"Ben?" she asked. "Don't you have to wear glasses when you work?"

"I can see you with my eyes closed."

"But can you see the canvas?"

"Let me worry about that."

"The clock is ticking," she reminded him.

"This isn't going to work if you sit there looking so delectable. I doubt that I could even draw a stick figure." Deliberately, he wiped his hands on a rag.

"Back to work," she said, recognizing the glint in his eyes.

"How about a break?"

"You don't need a break. You haven't done anything yet."

"I've been setting up the composition in my mind."

"That doesn't count."

"Trust me to take up with a temperamental woman," he muttered. Breathing a long sigh, he picked up his chalk and stared at the canvas. "There you go again."

"There I go again, what?"

"Wiggling your toes. It drives me wild."

"I'm wearing shoes. How can you tell?"

"There you go again," he repeated, after another moment. "Are you trying to seduce me?"

"I didn't wiggle my toes."

"This time you wiggled your ear."

"I didn't."

"Behave yourself or I won't be responsible for what happens."

When the last strains of the Chopin nocturne died, silence filled the room as another record was automatically dropped onto the turntable. Arley didn't recognize the music, but it was soft and plaintive. It made her think of grassy meadows and wildflowers, and two people in love walking hand in hand, lost in the delight.

Or would any music—from Mozart to Michael Jackson—have made her feel that way, now that she and Ben were together again? Would she need music at all?

Had he read her mind? He didn't say anything this time when he set his chalk down. He simply came toward her.

"What's wrong?" she asked, trying to sound firm. "Why aren't you working?"

"I will. But I have to kiss you. Just once. For sustenance."

"I thought creating was an artist's sustenance."

"Not this artist."

"One kiss?" she repeated.

If their foolish exchange—and the pretense of playing artist and model—had been designed to keep distance between them while they learned more about each other, it wasn't working. Any resistance Arley had brought with her in the name of common sense had deserted her.

"One—to start," he said, sensing victory.

"One," she agreed breathlessly when he was beside her, bending down, his breath teasing her lips.

The room around them spun and shrunk. Colors and textures merged. Except for their heartbeats, all sounds faded and died away.

"Arley? Are you in there?" someone called. It was Suzette. She was at the door to Ben's apartment. "Arley!"

"We won't answer." Ben touched a finger to her lips, where his mouth should have been.

"Trav?" Suzette persisted, knocking now. "Trav, is Arley with you?"

"I don't think she's going to give up." With a groan, he straightened and with a firm hand on her shoulder, indicated that Arley should stay put. "Remember where we left off. I'll take care of this."

He flung open the door. "I'm sorry to bother you, but there's somebody here to..." Suzette began, then noting the fierce expression on his face, finished weakly, "... to see Arley."

Arley slid off the stool, causing the scarf to fall to the floor, and she stooped to retrieve it. "I'm not expecting anyone tonight."

Mildred Barnes was a few feet behind Suzette, struggling to control a shaggy gray-and-white dog who looked as if he outweighed her by about seventy-five pounds. "This is Rags," Mildred said, breathless from exertion. "I know you said I should meet you in the alley tomorrow at the crack of dawn, but my building manager was raising hell. He said Rags had been howling and whining the whole time I was gone, disturbing the other tenants."

"Howling?" Ben said.

"It wasn't true," Mildred insisted firmly. "It was just an excuse to get Rags off the premises. He hates dogs. You know the kind."

"This is *little* Rags?" Ben asked.

"Yes. Isn't he a dear? I wish I could keep him. But you know these no-pet jerks. What can I do?" Mildred smoothed the fur away from the dog's face, but it flopped back again. She handed the leash to Arley and pointed to the large sack of kibble, two plastic dishes and the mesh bag full of assorted dog toys that sat on the ground nearby. "Those are his things. You'll never know how hard it was to drive over here with him in the back seat. At least, he started in the back seat. By the way, if you keep him supplied with giant-size biscuits, he won't chew the legs off your coffee table."

"The coffee table?" Ben echoed.

"I gotta go now." Mildred walked backward toward the street. "I'm parked in a No Parking zone. I'll be in touch in a few days. Keep your fingers crossed that I can find a home for him."

"I will," Arley said, not daring to ask about the family that Mildred had hoped would take Rags. Apparently, another landlord vetoed pets. "Believe me I will."

"And thanks a lot."

"So this is little Rags," Ben said, when Mildred had gone.

"He's much littler inside all that fur," Suzette offered, helpful as always.

"When she said 'little,'" Arley commented, "I suppose she didn't actually mean he was small. You know—'poor little thing' can apply to, well, King Kong."

"Then I guess we're lucky there, aren't we?" Ben thrust out one arm. "Hey, get him away from... He's digging at the roots of that fern."

"Oops." Arley tugged at the leash, but to no avail. "He isn't really digging—he's just sniffing. I guess he wants to get the lay of the land."

"Well, judging by that hole, we must have gophers."

"Oh, dear, he's got dirt all over his paws, too," Suzette obligingly pointed out. "You'd better clean it off before you take him upstairs, or you're going to need to clean that gorgeous new carpet."

"Here." Ben stepped forward, holding out his hand. "He's going to pull your arm off. Let me take the leash."

Growling deep in his throat, Rags bared strong, white teeth.

Ben yanked his hand back. "Great. I told you dogs don't like me. This one is no exception."

"He's very gentle," Arley said, stooping down to look into what she thought were the dog's eyes—there was too much hair over them to be sure. "And he likes you. He likes everybody, see? Your shouting frightened him. Remember, he's been abused."

"Are you sure it wasn't Rags that did the abusing?"

"Speak to him softly before you try to pet him," she said. "Let him know you don't mean him any harm."

Ben squared his shoulders. "This isn't easy for either of us, pal," he told the dog. "One of your kind bit me once."

"Call him by his name," Arley prodded.

"Hello, Rags," Ben said quietly. "You're with friends now. Nobody's going to hurt you."

This time the pup's growl was more halfhearted, and he sat perfectly still. Then, whimpering, he lowered himself to the sidewalk and inched forward to rest his muzzle on Ben's shoe.

"Oh, isn't that sweet?" Suzette cooed. "He wasn't growling at you, Trav. That was just his way of saying hello."

"You speak dog?" Grudgingly, Ben leaned down to scratch the pup's ear.

Seemingly overjoyed by this overture of friendship, Rags leapt up and planted his paws on Ben's shirt, streaking it with dirt.

"No, no, boy," Arley scolded, tugging at the leash.

"Hey, what have we here?" Jonathan called from his doorway. "The new tenant? Make sure he reads the rules before he signs the lease, Travis."

"Let's go, Rags." Arley said, sensing that Ben's anger was about to surface. She gave the chain another pull as the dog started investigating Ben's ferns again. "Don't you want to see your new home? Temporary home?" she added quickly for Ben's benefit.

Keeping several feet behind her, Ben followed her up the stairs. "What about the kittens? They'd each be just a bite for him."

Arley had been worried about that, too. "He won't hurt them, I'm sure. Mildred said he's used to other animals. But I'll keep them separated until they get to know each other."

"Want me to take Samson and Delilah over to Dora's until Rags gets his bearings?" Suzette asked.

"Would you?"

"Sure."

Delilah, who'd been sleeping when they came in, was easy for Suzette to scoop up. Samson, however, struggled out of her grasp almost at once. When he spied Rags, his fur stood on end, making him look twice his size. Obviously deciding that the best offense was a good defense, he arched his back and hissed.

Rags emitted a series of high-pitched yelps and retreated. Running in circles, he tangled himself and Ben in the chain, eventually settling between Ben's feet.

"Oh, poor thing," Suzette said. "He's so frightened."

"How are you planning to manage this menagerie?" Ben asked Arley, trying to extricate himself from the chain while the puppy exuberantly licked his hand.

"As you can see, Rags won't hurt the kittens." Arley's smile was forced as she tried for a confident tone. "Suzette's going to help. And I'm sure Dora and Caroline will, too. When I'm at work, the kittens will be with them and I'll keep Rags in the kitchen with lots of toys and biscuits."

"To prevent him from chewing the legs off your coffee table," Ben said grimly.

"He only needs to feel loved."

"I like your headgear, Travis," Jonathan snickered as he came up the stairs. Pretending to be interested in the dog, he stood beside Suzette.

Without commenting, Ben ripped off the beret.

"What's his name?" Jonathan asked.

"Rags," Suzette said archly, moving to one side to put room between them.

"He's a cute one, isn't he?" Jonathan smiled brightly at Suzette.

"Oh, you think so? He's got mud on his paws. Doesn't that make him a slob in your book?" Suzette asked too sweetly.

"Can you hold him here while I get a cloth to clean the dirt off?" Arley asked, holding the leash out to Jonathan.

"Er, you hold him, I'll get the cloth," he said, shrinking away as if she'd offered him a snake.

"The spider sprang," Ben said under his breath when Suzette had taken the kittens and Jonathan had gone.

"What?"

"Where does it end, Arley? Do you always say what I want to hear, reserving the truth until it's convenient?"

"I told you about Rags," she said, struggling to control the puppy.

"Little Rags? Gentle Rags? No wonder you tried to keep me from meeting him."

"I didn't," she protested.

"No? Didn't you make arrangements with Ms. Barnes to meet you in the alley tomorrow before I'd be up and about? Did you actually think you could keep him a secret?"

"I made those arrangements before you and I talked."

"Uh-huh." His tone conveyed his disbelief.

"It'll only be for a few days."

"How long did it take Rome to burn?" He shot back. "Besides, didn't I hear her tell you to keep your fingers crossed that she'd find a home for him?"

"Yes, but—"

"Does that mean she expects you to keep him here until she does?"

"I don't know. Once I get Rags settled, I'll call her and make her understand that this is temporary."

"Temporary means a few days. I'll hold you to that."

"I know."

Evidently feeling left out, the pup whimpered and looked up at Ben through his mop of gray-and-white hair.

"Let's not discuss it now." Ben seemed more tired than angry. He reached down to give Rags's shaggy head a pat, to which Rags responded with hearty tail-wagging. "I'd better get back to work. I've wasted too much time already."

"Don't worry about this," Arley said.

"I'm not," he muttered, turning away. "It's your problem. Handle it."

CHAPTER TWELVE

IT WAS PAST NINE before the animals were settled—Rags in the kitchen, the kittens in the bedroom—and Arley could get to the market. One of the clerks obligingly found a large box exactly the right size for Rags and squeezed it into her car. Now that she was home, all she had to do was get it out without crushing the sides.

Looking up, she saw that the moon was the round, yellow face depicted in her childhood storybooks. Tonight the darkish spots on the surface actually formed features. But darned if those features didn't appear more grim than happy. Or was she only seeing a reflection of what she was feeling?

"Here, let me take that," Ben said, stepping out of the night so unexpectedly she almost cried out.

"No, thanks. It isn't heavy. It's just awkward." She shifted the box to her other side, allowing them to walk up side by side comfortably.

"More strawberries," he said, indicating the grocery bag he was carrying. "I polished the others off last night."

"With sugar and cream?"

"Straight from the box, like potato chips. But better for me."

"That's true. Without all that salt." Arley thought for a moment. How much more conversation could they wring from a box of strawberries? "I've just come from the market, too. I didn't see you."

"It's a pretty night. I felt like walking."

"I needed a bed for Rags. I figured if I cut this box down and put a couple of blankets inside, it should do nicely."

"I doubt he cares what he sleeps in, as long as it's comfortable."

"Especially since it's only temporary," she added quickly.

Ben was wearing a long-sleeved gray shirt of a coarse weave. In the moonlight, his nose and cheekbones were sharply defined, making her think of the strong, silent heroes in cowboy movies. She wouldn't have been too surprised if he called her "ma'am" and said "Smile when you say that."

"You're sure that box is empty?" he asked.

Given the turn of her thoughts, she didn't realize at first that he was teasing her about the last box she'd brought home. The one filled with kittens. "Want to look?"

"I'll take your word for it."

Would he really?

Earlier he'd asked her if she always said what he wanted to hear, reserving the truth until it was convenient. Would he ever trust her again?

As they reached the stairs, she started up, but his smile—though faint—along with his effort to be friendly, gave her the courage to ask a question that needed asking.

"I've boiled the potatoes," she said. "Should I go ahead and make potato salad?"

"That's rich. You ask my permission to make potato salad, but when it comes to important things, you do as you damn well please."

She shifted the box to her other hip. "I'd hoped you weren't angry anymore."

"I'm not."

"You could have fooled me."

His gaze swung across the street to where a motorcycle had just started up. "I didn't mean that like it sounded."

"If our lunch date is off for tomorrow, I won't make salad. I'll...cut the potatoes into cubes and freeze them for home fries." She walked up two stairs and stopped, letting the box rest against the railing briefly when it began to slip. "Maybe I'd better do that anyway."

"Don't be so touchy."

"I only want to know where we stand," she said. "With our plans tomorrow, I mean."

"Are you saying it's up to me?" He sounded incredulous. "I'd have thought it was up to the four-legged guys—they're the ones who run the joint now. Can you actually get away for a few hours?"

"Everything's under control," she said, deciding that in the face of things, he was entitled to a modicum of sarcasm. "Suzette's promised to look in on them occasionally."

If her words gave him confidence, it wasn't mirrored in his smile. "Then I guess we're on for tomorrow."

She took an extra breath as a small surge of excitement passed through her, and she realized for the first time how important he'd become to her in the short time they'd known each other.

Things would be all right between them. She'd make them all right tomorrow.

"Good." She attempted to sound carefree. "I'll send my car for you at about noon."

"Hold it," he called, as she reached the landing. "Dinner. In the middle of the day?"

"Millions of people all over the country eat then. Only they call it lunch."

"Hmm. I've heard of it." He nudged a stray pebble off the sidewalk with his toe. "But my best appetite doesn't wake up until the sun goes down."

"Give it a try." She smiled. "You might like it."

No DOUBT ANTICIPATING a fancy meal, with dainty china, candlelight, and Arley floating about in peach chiffon, Ben looked less than enthusiastic the next day when she appeared, dressed in white shorts and a yellow-and-white gingham shirt.

A brief description of the delicacies that filled the wicker basket, including chocolate cake and her famous homemade potato salad, didn't help much.

"I never did like eating outside," he complained, still showing his disappointment as they weighed down the tablecloth with stones and settled themselves in the dappled shade of a willow. "I suppose it's because whenever I do so at my sister's house, there are always steaks on the grill, and her husband is always in his chef's hat asking me how I want mine. They usually give me the honor of tossing the salad."

"And you don't like that."

"I like to be waited on," he teased, reminding her of that first day in his apartment when he'd accused her of having a princess complex.

"I'll wait on you," she promised.

"Brushing the sand off the sandwiches? Waving the flies away from the lemonade?"

"I'm sorry you're disappointed," she said, wondering if she should fold everything up again, chuck it into the trunk of her car and drive them to a restaurant.

"Hey." Flashing one of the endearing smiles she was beginning to think she'd never see again, he caught her hand and pressed it to his lips. "Don't pay any attention to me. I think it's a great idea."

"Really?"

"Sure. I like ants and noise and kids tripping over my feet."

She laughed. "I thought you would."

Mustering some interest, he lifted the cover of the basket and peered inside. "Is that a checkerboard I spy?"

"How observant of you. It is."

"I haven't played checkers since I was twelve."

"Then prepare to be soundly beaten."

"Not hardly. Some things you never forget."

He won the first game of checkers, as he'd predicted, but blatantly threw the second to her. He shouldn't have. She won the third on her own, giving her two out of three.

After eating, they walked, tried out the slides and swings, then sat on the grass again, talking, and watching the people around them.

When, as the afternoon wore on, a dog-obedience class started nearby, Ben slapped a hand to his forehead. "Don't tell me you got the parks-and-recreation people to arrange this."

"Not guilty. Do you want to move?" she asked with exaggerated concern.

"It's okay. As long as we don't have to take any of the performers home with us."

It was fun watching the circle of owners with their pets being put through their paces. Even Ben clapped at the end of each drill and laughed, along with other onlookers, when an apricot-colored poodle, the clown of the bunch, kept trying to hide behind a trash bin.

Apparently relaxed by the entertainment, Ben told Arley a few things he hadn't bothered to explain before. He spoke of a small inheritance he'd received from his grandfather's estate when he was twenty-five. According to the will, Ben was to use the money to invest in real estate, because his grandfather had felt that was the way to security.

It was enough for a down payment on an apartment building that, though rather run-down, was located in a good section of the city. Ben had worked at two jobs to make enough money to do the million and one things necessary to make the place habitable.

Too young to know any better, he'd made no demands of his tenants and set no rules at all. Proud of the building, he wanted everyone to be happy there. The tenants' dogs, who spent their days ruining the carpets and scratching the woodwork and doors, spent their nights barking. The tenants' cats, who passed their days clawing the draperies to ribbons, passed their nights carrying on their territorial battles.

The reliable tenants, the few who didn't make trouble and paid their rent on time, finally moved out. The animal-control officer was a regular visitor and citations were frequent.

Finally, when Ben asked the guilty parties to leave, they stopped paying rent and he was forced to get the sheriff to evict them.

"You'd never believe the condition of that building. It looked like it had been in a war zone. To add insult to injury, a litter of kittens was left behind, and I had to find homes for them."

"How terrible."

"So now you know."

"I can understand your feelings." Arley paused. "But you could have avoided all that trouble if you'd interviewed your prospective tenants before you rented to them."

"How do you interview a Doberman?"

"Simple. You find out everything you want to know by talking with the owners. The people who don't have their pets fixed, or don't clean up after their animals, or let them run wild, are the same ones who allow their children to run through the flower beds, write on walls, litter the yard and clog the plumbing."

"Granted. But what if you don't have time to conduct those interviews?"

"Then you should invest in IBM or AT&T, not in people. When you become a landlord, you have a responsibility." As she spoke, her heart sank. She hadn't meant their day to end this way.

"Dammit, I resent being lectured. I've always considered myself easy-going. I like running the apartment building, and I think I do a pretty good job of making things comfortable for all concerned without stepping on anybody's toes.''

"You do," she admitted. "Mostly."

"Mostly. Now you come along and make me feel like the villain of the piece."

"I didn't mean to do that. I only wanted to show you the other side of the picture."

He thought a moment, then grinned sheepishly. "I guess I did need to see it, didn't I? I should have my head examined." Digging into the picnic basket, he pulled out a bread stick. "Maybe I should just eat and stay out of trouble."

"One more question before we drop the subject?"

He groaned and pointed the bread stick at her. "Just one."

"What do you have against goldfish?"

"Ah, yes. The fish. You're visualizing two or three innocuous little fish flitting here and there in a little round bowl, I imagine. Well, the fish in question came in two huge tanks. And those tanks weren't properly constructed. One had been patched with what appeared to be metallic tape."

"So?"

"So, once I had another tenant—"

"Another inconsiderate tenant?"

"Don't interrupt. This is the last time I'm going to explain my stand to you or—anyone. I had a tenant with a fish tank that broke while he was at work one day. Not only did the water wreck the carpet, it dripped through, ruined the ceiling plaster in the apartment underneath and damaged the finish on an antique cabinet."

"That's a once-in-a-lifetime happening."

"You're right. Once in *my* lifetime. And that's why I said no to the other guy."

"But—"

"You had your one question. That's it."

"Are you angry because I asked?"

He pressed his lips together, looked at the bread stick and dropped it back into the basket. "I don't want this."

"Are you? Angry, I mean?"

"I guess I was for a second there."

"Was?"

"The business about the fish has nothing to do with you and me." His voice was ragged. "Any more than it would if I decided to rent my apartments only to red-headed taxi drivers."

"And what would happen in the world if everyone decided to do that?"

"Then there'd be a lot of people with nowhere to go."

"My point exactly."

He stared at the sky in exasperation. "Except that we aren't talking about people here. We're talking about animals."

"And their owners, who come in all sizes, shapes and professions."

"I think it's time we went home." Not waiting for her to agree, he stood, brushed the grass off his khaki pants and began gathering up their picnic things.

"I wish our day hadn't ended in an argument," she said as they walked toward the car, an ache beginning at the back of her throat as she remembered that this was just a preview of coming attractions if Mildred didn't find a new home for Rags.

"I have a notion it won't be our last." Ben stopped walking and reached out to brush a strand of hair from her eyes. His tender touch told her that none of his anger remained.

"We're still friends?" she asked, as he settled her into the passenger seat of her car.

He got in the driver's side and slammed the door. "Nothing you say or do could make me stay angry with you for long."

"Will you put that in writing?" she asked, only half joking.

"Why? What mischief are you planning on next?"

"I don't know."

"You're asking for carte blanche?"

"Maybe."

"Let me think about it." He grunted. "Ready to go? I want to take the scenic route home. I have something to show you."

"There it is." Fifteen minutes later, Ben stopped in front of a circle of tumbledown cottages built around a Spanish-style courtyard. "See the wishing well?"

"I do," Arley said, thinking the well seemed to be in better shape than the cottages.

They were a faded aquamarine, and several windows were broken. The yard was hard-packed dirt with only a few tufts of crabgrass, most of it growing between the cracked stepping stones. Still, Ben was enthusiastic about these cottages, one of which he was thinking of buying, and she tried to see the potential he thought it had.

"My grandfather always told me, if you have your choice of buying a great house in a dying neighborhood or a hovel in a good one, you pick the hovel,"

Ben said. "You can turn the hovel into a place you can be proud of. But what good would Hearst's Castle be in an area where the land values have dropped and are still dropping?"

"What about the lakefront property you went to see?"

"It had possibilities. Peace and quiet, a spectacular view. At some other time, I'd jump at the chance."

"But not now?"

He bit his lower lip. "When I first considered it, I'd expected to live there and get someone to manage the units in town."

"And?"

"I decided it's too far from the city."

"But you don't commute. A free-lancer makes his office wherever he hangs his hat."

He grasped the steering wheel more tightly. "Are you trying to get rid of me?"

Did he mean, *could* he mean, that he would have been too far from her? She hardly dared to hope.

"It's going to take a lot of work," she said, turning her attention back to the cottages.

"I like a challenge." He stared at her for a long moment. "But I guess you know that already."

"You consider me a challenge?"

"Should I?"

"Not anymore," she said, the words popping out before she realized what she was saying. She didn't mind, though. They made him smile.

"What did you put in that lemonade?" he asked, his expression softening.

"Nothing. Not even lemons. It was canned concentrate. Why?"

"I've never wanted to kiss anyone as much as I want to kiss you right now."

The huskiness in his tone made her dizzy. "What's stopping you? Nobody's looking."

"No way. The next time I get you in my arms—" he turned the key in the ignition too hard, causing it to make a grating sound "—I intend to finish what I start."

When they got home, Arley was surprised to see that the bright sunlight of afternoon was changing into the soft purple of evening. The automatic lights in front of the building were already on.

How could time have flown by so quickly?

As she and Ben walked up the steps, neither of them spoke. This time there was no accompanying music from Jonathan's apartment. But they didn't need it.

Then, somewhere on the second level, a door slammed.

"I've already looked!" a woman cried. It sounded like Suzette.

"I'll try the alley again." It was a man this time. Jonathan? Yes. In his haste, he didn't appear to notice Arley and Ben as he passed them on the stairs.

"What's wrong?" Arley asked.

He stared at them, not answering, then he turned and raced back up the stairs calling, "They're home!"

"Oh, Arley." Suzette's metal-studded sandals clattered above them as she sped toward the stairwell. "You're never going to forgive me. Something frightful has happened!"

CHAPTER THIRTEEN

"THE KITTENS!" Arley cried, alarm ripping through her.

Had Rags become frantic at being penned in the kitchen and . . .

Not allowing the thought to take form, she pushed past Suzette and ran toward the wide-open door of her apartment.

"Samson and Delilah are fine," Suzette called after her. "It's Rags. He's gone."

"How could he be?"

"Don't start yelling at me. I didn't think he'd try to escape."

"What happened?"

"I'm afraid the fault can be placed at my doorstep," Jonathan said, nobility coloring his voice. He came up behind Suzette and put his hands on her shoulders. "I knew Suzette was cat-sitting in your apartment and that you'd be gone for a while. I thought it would be a good time for me to get things straightened out between us."

Rags had been whining, Suzette said, taking over the explanation. She'd been sitting on the floor beside his box, petting him and trying to make him feel at home when Jonathan knocked. She'd answered and, in the heat of their argument, forgot to fasten the kitchen door. Then the dog wandered into the living room, and Samson started acting up.

"He arched his back and came charging forward with all the ferocity he could muster. One look at him and Rags bolted into the hall."

"Didn't you go after him?" Arley asked, mentally planning her pursuit.

"Jonathan caught him by the collar, but Rags twisted out of it, and was down the stairs in seconds. Trav's window was open and he leapt through."

"My window," Ben echoed.

"Once he was in there, I thought I could corner him," Jonathan said, gesturing broadly, like a prize-fighter explaining one of his matches blow by blow. "But when I tried to climb into the apartment, there was a crash, and he jumped out again, right over my head."

"A crash," Ben repeated dully.

"It's okay," the insurance man said. "It was just your drawing table falling over. It made such a clatter I thought the worst, but I couldn't see any real damage. Only a lot of scattered papers."

Ben looked numb.

"Rags took off down the street," Suzette continued, "but I was barefoot and had to get my shoes. Jonathan had to go back and close your door so the kittens wouldn't get away, too."

"By then, Rags was nowhere in sight."

"Nobody's on night duty at the animal shelter who can conduct a search," Suzette said as Arley started for the phone. "We've already called."

Until a roar reverberated through the breezeway, Arley had thought Ben was still behind her. He wasn't. He'd gone to inspect the damage to his apartment.

"Damn!" he hollered. "This is all I need."

"Is something broken?" Fearfully, Arley flew down the stairs and peered through the open casement window.

As Jonathan had said, Ben's drawing table had been knocked over, scattering his work in progress and a rack that had held sketches, notebooks and other assorted papers. Jars of pencils, pens and brushes were on the floor, too, as well as textbooks—some with their pages ripped. Atop it all lay an overturned bottle of red ink.

The telephone lay nearby, emitting a high-pitched signal that could be heard across the room.

"Oh, Ben, I'm sorry," Arley said as he began setting things right.

"'Sorry' doesn't cut it." He indicated the jumble on the floor. "This represents countless hours of…of…"

"What a mess." Suzette looked in, wrinkling her nose.

"I apologize for my part in this, Travis," Jonathan began, "but if you kept your windows closed and enjoyed the benefits of air-conditioning like everybody else, it wouldn't have happened."

"Leave." Ben clenched his hands. "Please, leave me alone."

"I suppose we should go," Arley said quietly, "if we're going to find Rags."

Besides, she thought, it might be better if they all stayed out of sight until Ben cooled down. Maybe it wasn't really as bad as it looked. Maybe his basic drawings could be saved. Later, when Rags was back where he belonged, she would help him put things in order.

"We'll go north as far as Baxter Road," Jonathan said, pulling Suzette along. "Arley, you go south. No sense in all of us covering the same territory."

Up one street and down the other Arley drove, finding no sign of the missing dog. After half an hour, she decided to continue on foot, reasoning that she couldn't search for Rags and drive at the same time. It was possible she'd already passed the animal without realizing it.

So she walked, stopping before each house to look behind bushes, calling the dog's name softly, asking each passerby if they'd seen anything. No one had.

"If he's that big," one woman said, her eyes wide with alarm, "I hope I don't run into him."

"It's okay. He's very gentle."

"Why don't you people lock your animals up?" a man snarled. "You got no right letting your damn dogs run loose."

Finally she decided to stop for the night. Her feet throbbed, and every square inch of her ached. Rags could have been a mere ten feet away, and she wouldn't be able to see him. It was just too dark. The search would have to wait until tomorrow. But she had to wonder what might happen to the poor thing by then.

Though she'd never known him to work at night, Ben, his glasses in place, was at the window bent over the drawing table he'd set back where it belonged.

"I didn't have any luck," she said through the window when he didn't ask. "Were you able to salvage anything?"

"Nothing. In fact, my preliminary sketches are too mutilated to trust for accuracy. I'll have to go back to the medical center tomorrow to do more research."

"I'm sorry," she said again.

"I'll have to ask for a deadline extension—something I've never done before."

"Can I help?" Other than arranging his work area, he hadn't done much to clean up the mess in his living room. Tired as she was, she would have been glad to do it.

"I think you've done enough." He tapped a furious tattoo on the drawing board with his pencil.

"You're blaming me for what happened?"

"I'm blaming me. I made a big mistake. Now I'm paying for it." His expression was forbidding. "You're good at making speeches. Maybe you can explain to me why I shouldn't go back to my old policy."

"Are you talking about the no-pets policy?"

"I have enough to do just handling people." He tipped his head back and glared at the ceiling. "Everything was peaceful around here before."

"Before I moved in?"

"At least, people kept their animals behind closed doors."

If he meant what he said, how would the decision affect Lovey Bear and Pansy Puss? Samson and Delilah? And if he grudgingly allowed them to remain, how would it affect future tenants? Even more important, what did it say about Ben?

"You're upset. You don't mean that," she said.

"Don't I?"

"I understand how you must feel. What happened here tonight was terrible. If there was any way to change it, I would. But that's no reason to—"

"Don't preach to me, lady. I'm in no mood for it."

Their eyes met, but Arley felt no contact had been made. There was much more separating them than the windowed wall.

Her face felt flushed. "If you can blithely go back on your word—"

"I didn't make any promises."

"If you can blithely go back on your word," she repeated, louder this time, "I doubt that your heart was in it in the first place. It was only a gesture."

"Meaning?"

"Meaning you were only looking for a merit badge."

"That's what you think, is it?"

"You were against having animals here all along. Now you use the first excuse that comes along to welsh on your deal."

"My work might be a joke to you, but it's important to me."

"I've never said it was a joke. But plumbers have broken water mains sometimes."

"Plumbers?"

"Baseball players have losing streaks." She gestured broadly, as she tried to find other, more appropriate examples. "Writers have manuscripts that are accidently destroyed. I've had computer programs completely wiped out. Setbacks like this are part of everyone's life."

"This isn't just a setback. It's every artist's nightmare."

"I understand that. But you're being unfair."

"Unfair?" He pushed back his chair with deliberation, and went to the door. Opening it and stepping outside toward her, he said, "Any decision I make about running this place has nothing to do with you and me."

"Doesn't it?"

He waited, as if expecting her to say something more. "If it does, then we're looking at another truth. If I allow you to dictate my policies, then what I thought was happening between us isn't all it seems."

"Maybe it isn't," she agreed after what seemed an interminable silence.

Was that all he saw in their argument? Arley trying to force her will on him? Overcome with outrage, she planned to put an exclamation point on their conversation by walking away without another word, but he went back inside and closed the door before she could manage it.

Wanting nothing more than to be alone with her dismal thoughts, Arley was disappointed to discover that Suzette was in her apartment waiting for her.

"You didn't find Rags, either?" The girl was wearing a knee-length belted robe of gray silk. Her hair was pinned on top of her head as if she'd just stepped out of the shower. "Want a cold pop?"

Arley shook her head.

"We drove for a while, but Jonathan thought we could do better on foot."

"Me, too," Arley said, trying to erase the image of Ben's angry face from her mind.

"He said we should try to think like Rags would, then maybe we could find where he was hiding."

"I'd ask for a sick day tomorrow," Arley said, groaning as she stepped out of her shoes. She'd developed a blister on the back of one foot. "But my appointment calendar is jammed. What about you?"

"I have to go in. My sick days are used up. Mind if I have something to drink? My throat is parched. All that racing around."

"As long as it's for the road. I can't remember ever being this tired."

"Don't worry. Rags will turn up."

"Do you really think so?" Arley needed to hear something optimistic, even if it wasn't sincere.

"Jonathan said we shouldn't feel bad about not being successful tonight. When dogs run like that, they don't stop. They go on and on. Rags could be miles away—downtown, or across the bridge into Illinois. There are an awful lot of shelters to check."

"Jonathan really knows how to cheer people up," Arley said, trying not to picture poor Rags, running and running, thirsty and afraid.

Had she been too hard on Ben? Maybe it had been only the anger of the moment talking. She should have waited until he'd cooled down before discussing anything.

"I have to tell you what happened." Suzette took a long drink of her orange pop. "When we got to this alley behind Grimshaw, we heard barking. It sounded like one dog resenting another dog trespassing on his territory."

"Was it Rags?"

"We looked over the fence," Suzette went on, not to be rushed, "and there was this big, shaggy dog. It's hard to see colors at night."

"Was it Rags?" Arley asked again.

"We thought so. Jonathan tried to squeeze through an opening between the wood and the wire, but he couldn't. So he climbed the fence, calling Rags's name. You should have seen him."

"What happened?"

"It wasn't Rags at all. It was this fierce monster of an animal who tried to make a meal of Jonathan. He barely made it back over the fence before the yard lights came on. I guess people thought we were prowlers. A man ran out of the house hollering, and we had to run for it." Suzette leaned against the door and laughed. "It was great."

"Great?"

"The sprinklers were on in the yard we crossed to make our getaway. Jonathan's sweater was already dirty from the fall he'd had trying to get over the fence, and the dirt turned to mud. His slacks were ripped where they'd snagged on the fence. He scuffed his shoes, too, and tore the fringed tassel off one of them."

"I'm sorry about that."

"The wonderful part is that he didn't even mention any of the damage. He didn't seem to care." Suzette smiled, and took another drink of pop. "I was so proud of him."

"I'm glad. Now, I'd really like to get ready for bed."

"I started thinking," Suzette continued, ignoring Arley. "Jonathan deals with the public in his job. A man has to look well dressed and prosperous, doesn't he, to convince people he knows what he's doing? Insurance is his chosen field, and he has a certain image to maintain. That's why he has to be so particular about his appearance.''

''Suzette—'' Arley felt as if there were sand behind her eyelids ''—I'd like to get some sleep tonight, if you don't mind.''

''But when it really counted—'' Suzette started for the door ''—when that dog's welfare was at stake, he didn't care how he looked. It couldn't have mattered less. Isn't he marvelous?''

''Good night,'' Arley said.

''If you want my opinion,'' Suzette added, stopping Arley from closing the door, ''Ben behaved like a jerk. He can always do those stupid drawings of his over. But did he think about that? No. He just shut himself in his apartment without even trying to help find Rags, while Jonathan was out trying to bring the pup home safely.''

''Good night, Suzette,'' Arley said again, helping her friend on her way with a light push on the shoulder.

When at last she was alone, she turned off the lights and started the water in the bathtub. A shower would have been faster and, under the circumstances, much more practical, but she needed the comforting sensation of being immersed in hot water, with steam soothing away the tension.

She wasn't sure she accepted Suzette's interpretation of Jonathan's actions, she thought, as she closed her eyes and relaxed in the water. He might not have said anything about his ruined wardrobe to Suzette—

what would he have gained?—but behind closed doors, he was probably weeping into his pillow.

It was much like Ben pretending to accept the existence of the pet underground. It was all a pose. A desire to score points.

Wasn't it?

CHAPTER FOURTEEN

THE TEN O'CLOCK conference couldn't be postponed, a brief telephone call told Arley. Two of those involved had flown in from Jefferson City expressly for the purpose of meeting her. If the proceedings ran longer than anticipated, she would even be hard-pressed to make it to Normandy Junior High for the introduction of the new computers. She couldn't beg off that one, either.

Any way she looked at it, she wouldn't be free to conduct another search for Rags until three o'clock. How many shelters would she be able to visit before closing time? As Suzette and Jonathan had so kindly pointed out, there were a lot.

As the day's activity had called for more business-like attire than usual—a navy blue suit, cream blouse buttoned to the neck and her taupe dress shoes—she'd lose more time by going home first to change.

Having no desire to clash with Ben again, when she finally arrived home, she parked her car in the garage, hoping to get in and out without seeing him.

"Arley," Ben called from above her.

He was on the roof again, shirtless, with his tool belt around his hips and a hammer in his hand. "Wait. I have to talk to you."

She averted her eyes and kept walking, berating herself for the ache beginning in her throat. "I can't talk now. I'm in a hurry. Make a list of your grievances against me, and I'll read them all later."

"Dammit, wait."

"Is that an order?" she called back, not slowing her pace.

With a bearlike growl, Ben clattered down the ladder, sliding the last few rungs in his haste, and made it to the landing just as she did. He caught her sleeve. "You don't have to go anywhere."

"I do. Let me go." She wriggled free, but he caught her again.

"No, you don't." He looked down into her face with dark, serious eyes. "Rags is here."

She threw a hand to her mouth. Her knees felt weak and almost buckled as the tension in her limbs evaporated. "Oh, thank goodness. He found his way back?"

"Not exactly."

"I want to see him," she said. "Is he all right?"

"Not exactly."

"What do you mean, not exactly?" Her chest seemed to be on fire.

"I wanted to prepare you," he said, drawing the words out, as he tightened his grip on her arm to keep her from dashing up the stairs. "He was hit by a car."

"Oh, no!"

"Take it easy. He's going to be fine. He's bandaged up, but nothing's broken."

"How? When?"

"This morning Suzette called Mildred Barnes about Rags, and Mildred checked the shelters. The one in

Pine Lawn had been contacted by an emergency veterinary clinic, about a dog that fit Rags's description. She identified him and came to talk to you. I tried you at work, but you were gone and no one knew how to reach you.''

''I don't understand how he got back here.''

''I went down and got him.''

''You?''

''They'd given him an injection to keep him from going into shock, and the poor little guy was woozy, but he wagged his tail when he saw me.''

''Poor *little* guy?'' Arley didn't know what to make of Ben's change in attitude.

''I petted him and he licked me—imagine that. Hurt as he was. It made me feel like an old friend.'' He grinned, remembering.

''Oh, Ben, thank you!''

''They'd planned to keep him overnight, but I thought—and the doctor agreed—that since he knew me, he'd do better in familiar surroundings.''

''Familiar surroundings,'' she echoed. ''He'd only been here a few hours.''

''Sometimes it doesn't take very long to know someone's on your side.''

''I suppose that's true,'' she said softly, wondering if his words had a double meaning or if she was reading more into them. ''May I see him?''

Ben pressed his lips together, considering her request.''I don't know. He's sleeping. We don't want to get him excited.''

''I'll be quiet.''

''I hope you don't mind. But I got the box out of your apartment and fixed him up in my kitchen.'' Ben spoke in a half whisper, the way he might in a hospital, as she trailed him down the breezeway to his apartment. He opened the door to allow her in first. "I thought it would make him more comfortable than the floor. Hey..."

The box was empty, but after a quick look around, they found the dog in Ben's bedroom, sleeping peacefully in the middle of a log-cabin-style quilt. His left front paw was heavily bandaged and a place had been shaved on his backside.

Arley tensed for Ben's roar of protest.

"That's a good sign," Ben said, not seeming to mind, "his making it onto the bed with that bad leg."

"Yes, it is," she said, still puzzled by his reaction as they crept out of the room and partially closed the door.

"Mildred said that a home has opened up for him. The one she told you about." Keeping his voice low, Ben led her across the room and outside.

"Thank heaven," Arley murmured, wondering if it was possible that things would go right for a change. "If the people can't come for him, I'll gladly deliver him tomorrow. That is, if he's well enough to ride by then and you don't mind him staying here tonight."

"I'm not so sure." Ben scratched his head. "This family has three kids. All under eight. Rags might not be up to it—considering what he's been through already in his life. The doctor said he's hardly grown. Not more than a year old."

"Oh?" Her pulses quickened. Did that mean he would allow her to keep the dog until a more suitable home was found for him? Still, to be fair, she had to tell him how long that might take, given the surplus pet population. "You may be right. As soon as he wakes up, I'll have Suzette help me get him back upstairs."

Ben's stared at her in disbelief. "And have him terrorized by that cat of yours? Forget it."

She could hardly contain her laughter. "Terrorized by Samson?"

He held up one hand, palm toward her. "Rags isn't a coward. Far from it. But what's he supposed to do when he's attacked by something as tiny as that kitten?"

"Did you say—attacked?"

"He had two choices. Let the kitten scratch him or stand up for himself and end up a villain. He couldn't win." Ben raised an eyebrow. "Believe me, I know the feeling."

"Do you?" Was he comparing himself to Rags and Arley to Samson?

"So he did the only other thing left open to him," Ben went on. "He ran."

"Are you trying to tell me something? Are you thinking of keeping Rags? Of making him *your* dog?"

"He is my dog. I bought a license that says so." He pulled a receipt out of his pocket and tapped it against his hand.

"Oh, Ben." There were any number of things she could have said. "Thank you," for instance, but that didn't sound right. Or, "What you're doing is wonderful." Then there was always, "I'll make it up to you."

"I love you," she said, instead.

The changing expressions on his face reminded her of the spinning wheel on a TV game show, impossible to read or predict. "You're only saying that because

I've decided to allow pets," he replied, after chewing on her declaration for what seemed like an eternity.

He was joking. That meant the wheel had stopped at "jackpot," didn't it? Or was he like the smooth game-show host who smiled pleasantly when the wheel stopped on "bankruptcy"?

"You know better than that," she chided softly.

"Prove it." His eyes challenged hers. The message behind them could have been anything.

"Any ideas how I should go about it?"

"You're the one with the ideas."

Sweet turmoil zigzagged through her, felling inhibitions in its wake. Collecting herself, she stepped toward him, kissed the base of his throat, then rested her cheek against his chest.

"That's it? That's supposed to convince me?"

"It's a start."

"Hmm."

"I might do better if you offered a few encouraging words."

"Such as 'I love you, too'?"

She nodded.

He tilted his head to one side. "I can't say it just like that. The mood has to be right."

"What did you have in mind?"

"Oh, a tantalizing spaghetti dinner. Candlelight. Mantovani on the stereo."

"Your place or mine?" she asked impishly.

"Yours. When I bought the carpet, the man talked me into buying an extra-thick underpad. He told me it would be comfortable enough to sleep on. I'd like to see for myself."

"Oh, really. To get back to what we were talking about a minute ago," she said, deciding to redirect the conversation, "you mean, basically you require a romantic atmosphere to enable you to express yourself?"

He smiled. "Basically, yes. That's what I mean."

"I believe I can handle that—now that the cat is out of the bag."

"So to speak."

She rose on tiptoe and kissed his lower lip, then outlined it with the tip of her tongue. Knowing she was the cause of the shudder that coursed through him sent her spirits soaring. The two of them stood together, their arms around each other, neither of them wanting to let the other go. How wonderful it was, she thought. For the first time to have no secrets between them. That was how it would stay.

"One more thing," she said timidly.

He grunted. "I'm afraid to ask."

"The word 'small'."

"Small? What about it?"

"Small Pets Considered. What are people supposed to do with their Great Danes, their German shepherds, their Dobermans?"

"Arley!" He shook a finger at her.

"Be fair. You have a big dog, after all."

"I own the joint."

"But look at Rags, for example. Big dogs are usually gentle," she inserted quickly, "and if they've been properly trained, they're no more trouble than small ones."

He answered with a shake of his head, followed by a shrug of defeat. "Okay. Are you sure you don't want me to add Elephants Welcome?"

"Oh, no," she said, feeling as Delilah must, when she was so content she purred. "I'm against anyone having exotic pets. Wild animals belong in the wild."

"Thank heaven for that, at least." Sighing in mock relief, Ben wound both arms around her to draw her closer still. "I hope you realize that you've taken on another job."

"What job is that?"

"Somebody has to rent Nordoff's apartment. Interviewing pet owners was your idea. You do it."

"Gladly."

"Do a good job of it, and we might talk about making it permanent."

"Interviewing?"

"Interviewing and acting as my model. The serious painting I plan to do, remember? The painting of you I started before Rags came into our life."

"You want me to model for you?"

"Among other things. Depending on whether you think you can tolerate being married to a man who goes for days without saying a word when he's working and growling at the slightest interruption."

"Hmm." Despite the song in her heart that threatened to burst forth, she frowned and pretended to consider this a rather unpalatable-sounding offer.

"On the plus side," he continued, "it would insure you against eviction, no matter what kind of squirrelly things you do."

The curtains moved in one of the upstairs apartments. Dora Shelby's smiling face appeared, and for

Arley's benefit, she held up one hand with the fingers making a V for victory.

Ben, not missing it, returned the woman's V with one of his own. "What do you say we check out that carpet now?"

"What about the spaghetti dinner and Mantovani?"

"Let's improvise," he said.

Deciding to wait until next week to present him with Dora's plan for setting aside a fenced exercise area for pets, she wove her arm through his. "Yes, let's," she said.

Take 4 bestselling love stories FREE

Plus get a FREE surprise gift!

Special Limited-time Offer

Mail to Harlequin Reader Service®

3010 Walden Avenue
P.O. Box 1867
Buffalo, N.Y. 14269-1867

YES! Please send me 4 free Harlequin Romance® novels and my free surprise gift. Then send me 6 brand-new novels every month, which I will receive months before they appear in bookstores. Bill me at the low price of $2.24 each plus 25¢ delivery and applicable sales tax if any*. That's the complete price and—compared to the cover prices of $2.99 each—quite a bargain! I understand that accepting the books and gift places me under no obligation ever to buy any books. I can always return a shipment and cancel at any time. Even if I never buy another book from Harlequin, the 4 free books and the surprise gift are mine to keep forever.

116 BPA AJJD

Name	(PLEASE PRINT)	
Address	Apt. No.	
City	State	Zip

This offer is limited to one order per household and not valid to present Harlequin Romance® subscribers.
*Terms and prices are subject to change without notice. Sales tax applicable in N.Y.

UROM-93R   ©1990 Harlequin Enterprises Limited

Fifty red-blooded, white-hot, true-blue hunks from every State in the Union!

Beginning in May, look for MEN MADE IN AMERICA! Written by some of our most popular authors, these stories feature fifty of the strongest, sexiest men, each from a different state in the union!

Two titles available every other month at your favorite retail outlet.

In July, look for:

CALL IT DESTINY by Jayne Ann Krentz (Arizona)
ANOTHER KIND OF LOVE by Mary Lynn Baxter (Arkansas)

In September, look for:

DECEPTIONS by Annette Broadrick (California)
STORMWALKER by Dallas Schulze (Colorado)

You won't be able to resist MEN MADE IN AMERICA!

THREE UNFORGETTABLE HEROINES
THREE AWARD-WINNING AUTHORS

MAVERICK HEARTS

A unique collection of historical short stories that capture the spirit of America's last frontier.

HEATHER GRAHAM POZZESSERE—over 10 million copies of her books in print worldwide
Lonesome Rider—The story of an Eastern widow and the renegade half-breed who becomes her protector.

PATRICIA POTTER—an author whose books are consistently Waldenbooks bestsellers
Against the Wind—Two people, battered by heartache, prove that love can heal all.

JOAN JOHNSTON—award-winning Western historical author with 17 books to her credit
One Simple Wish—A woman with a past discovers that dreams really do come true.

Join us for an exciting journey West with
UNTAMED
Available in July, wherever Harlequin books are sold.